READ ME
ANOTHER STORY

COMPILED BY THE CHILD STUDY
ASSOCIATION OF AMERICA

READ-TO-ME STORYBOOK

READ ME ANOTHER STORY

READ ME MORE STORIES

HOLIDAY STORYBOOK

READ TO YOURSELF STORYBOOK

MORE READ TO YOURSELF STORIES
Fun and Magic

CASTLES AND DRAGONS
Read-to-Yourself Fairy Tales
for Boys and Girls

READ TO ME AGAIN

NOW YOU CAN READ TO YOURSELF

ROUND ABOUT THE CITY

READ ME
ANOTHER STORY

Compiled by the Child Study Association
of America

Illustrated by Barbara Cooney

NEW YORK: THOMAS Y. CROWELL COMPANY

Acknowledgments

For the privilege of reprinting the following copyrighted poems and stories, grateful acknowledgment and thanks are extended to the publishers indicated:

Leona Adelson, *The Blowaway Hat*, reprinted by permission of the David McKay Company, publisher.

Grace and Olive Barnett, *Egbert Learns To Quack*, reprinted by permission of the authors.

Dorothy W. Baruch, *Christmas Stocking*, reprinted by permission of Young Scott Books, publisher.

Erick Berry, *A Pretty Little Doll*, copyright 1946 by Oxford University Press, reprinted by permission of the publisher.

Irma Simington Black, "New Shoes" from *Pictures and Stories*, copyright by Pierce and Smith, reprinted by permission.

Tony Brice, *Little Bobo and His Blue Jacket*. Copyright 1944 by Rand McNally & Company, Publishers.

Margaret Wise Brown, *Little Chicken*, copyright 1943 by Harper & Brothers, reprinted by permission of the publisher.

Dorothy and Marguerite Bryan, *There Was Tammie!*, copyright 1935 by Dorothy M. Bryan, reprinted by permission of Dodd, Mead & Company, publisher.

Madye Lee Chastain, *Susan and the Rain*, reprinted by permission of Whitman Publishing Company, publisher.

Harriet Eager Davis, *Mother Knew*, reprinted by permission of the author.

Blanche Elliott, *Timothy Titus*, copyright 1937 by Doubleday & Company, Inc., reprinted by permission of the publisher.

Preface

"Read to me" is perhaps the most familiar, and the most recurrent, of all nursery chants. "Read me another story" follows close upon it. Children are insatiable listeners!

Young children demand their favorite stories over and over again. Along with these, however, they welcome new tales, which, in turn, are often quickly adopted into the inner circle of favorites, evoking from the small listener that highest of all tributes: "Read it again!"

Reading aloud, and being read to, are among the most treasured links between parent and child, to be deeply remembered and woven into the pattern of quiet togetherness. There is a special preciousness in the boom of father's voice, the comfort of mother's arm as the little one snuggles down to look as well as listen—to match the real pictures in the book with the "mind pictures" formed by the words.

We would like to think that the deep-rooted values of such a family hour might continue as the children grow up. Even when boys and girls can read for themselves, reading aloud by parents adds immeasurably to the warmth of family living and growing through the years. Especially in an era such as ours, with radio and television bringing, even to our littlest ones, experiences all too unselected for their needs, this intimate and personal sharing of reading acquires a double value, to be carefully nurtured by parents.

Stories such as those gathered here, in this second collection of Read-to-Me Stories, are a bridge from the shelter of home to the great world outside. New words, new patterns of thought, humor and fantasy widen the horizons of the youngest listener. These stories are the stuff of an astonishing world of new experiences: things and people, animals and insects, nature's phenomena and man-made contraptions.

It is the purpose of this collection to put between the covers a wide range of material which otherwise must be found in an assortment of separate books. Barbara Cooney's illustrations have added to each story a child-like grace, and brought unity to the whole.

The stories in this little volume have been thoughtfully selected by the Children's Book Committee of the Child Study Association of America, not only for the nursery listener but with an eye also on the beginning reader who welcomes easy yet interesting stories on which to try out his newly acquired skill. All of the Committee's members are parents; some are also children's librarians, teachers, or writers. All of their combined experiences and backgrounds have been focused on the selections in this anthology, testing and trying them out on children, on grandchildren, in homes, and in groups.

As always, the Committee gratefully acknowledges the guidance and unfailing good judgment of its staff adviser, Josette Frank.

In this undertaking, too, the Committee is particularly indebted to one of its members, Bella Koral, who has been indefatigable in her search for the "just right" story to fit each purpose. Her astonishing memory and fine discrimination have come to our aid again and again.

For all of the Committee this second venture into the realm of stories for the very youngest has been a delightful and a challenging task.

FLORA STRAUS
Chairman of the Children's Book Committee
Child Study Association of America

Contents

READ ME
ANOTHER STORY

THE STORY OF A LITTLE WHITE DOG

by DOROTHY SHERRILL

Once upon a time there was a little white dog.

He had shaggy white hair.

He had shiny brown eyes.

He had a funny floppy tail like a dish mop.

He lived in a big white house with a little boy named Peter and a little girl named Polly.

Every sunshiny day the little white dog played with Peter and Polly in the garden outside the house.

I

On rainy days he played with them in their playroom or on the big front porch.

When he got tired of playing he would curl up for a nap on his own special cushion in a corner of the porch.

When he got hungry he would eat out of his own special dish that was right next to his cushion. He ate cereal and small pieces of meat and puppy biscuit. Then a nice juicy bone for dessert.

He was a very happy little dog. His shiny brown eyes always looked as if they were laughing. His dish-mop tail wagged and wagged. When he barked, it was a woof-y, happy bark.

He was happy even when Peter and Polly had to go to morning kindergarten. Because then he would run races with butterflies in the garden. Or he would chase grasshoppers. Or he would

go out back of the house and watch the fluffy yellow chickens in the chicken yard.

At first he thought the chickens were butter-flies because they were yellow. He tried to get them to run races with him. But they hopped away and hid in the chicken house.

Then he thought maybe they were a new kind of grasshopper. He started to chase them. But Peter and Polly came home from kindergarten in time to see him. And they told him he must never, never chase chickens.

So after that he walked slowly when he was near the chickens. And if he barked he did it softly so as not to frighten them.

One day something exciting happened. The lit-tle white dog heard Peter and Polly's father say, "A fox tried to get into the chicken house last night. We'll have to buy a watch dog."

Peter said, "Our dog could be a watch dog. He is brave as a lion."

That made the little dog feel very proud. He wagged his tail waggle—waggle—waggle. He barked a big brave bark, "WOOF!"

But their father said, "Oh, he's too little. He wouldn't be any good."

That made the little dog feel unhappy. But he

Peter and Polly had given the dogs an extra special supper. The big dog gobbled his down. Then, the minute the children went back into the house, he pushed the little dog away and gobbled all that supper, too.

Every bit of it—except for one small bone!

Then the big dog stretched out for a nap—with his feet on the little dog's cushion, and the rest of him on his own.

The little dog took the one small bone and gnawed and gnawed on it.

He heard Peter and Polly go to bed upstairs.

He saw the stars begin to shine.

And still the big dog slept.

The little dog tried to sleep, too. But he couldn't because he was hungry.

It got later and later.

And then do you know what happened?

There was a sound out in the chicken house! A chicken squawked!

Quick as a flash the little dog ran down the porch steps. He flew faster than a butterfly or a grasshopper straight to the chicken yard.

He barked so loudly that he sounded almost like a lion!

Peter and Polly heard the barking. They came

go out back of the house and watch the fluffy yellow chickens in the chicken yard.

At first he thought the chickens were butter-flies because they were yellow. He tried to get them to run races with him. But they hopped away and hid in the chicken house.

Then he thought maybe they were a new kind of grasshopper. He started to chase them. But Peter and Polly came home from kindergarten in time to see him. And they told him he must never, never chase chickens.

So after that he walked slowly when he was near the chickens. And if he barked he did it softly so as not to frighten them.

One day something exciting happened. The lit-tle white dog heard Peter and Polly's father say, "A fox tried to get into the chicken house last night. We'll have to buy a watch dog."

Peter said, "Our dog could be a watch dog. He is brave as a lion."

That made the little dog feel very proud. He wagged his tail waggle—waggle—waggle. He barked a big brave bark, "WOOF!"

But their father said, "Oh, he's too little. He wouldn't be any good."

That made the little dog feel unhappy. But he

cheered up when he thought how nice it would be to have another dog to play with while Peter and Polly were in kindergarten.

So the little dog sat on the front porch all morning. And every time a car came along the road, he would wag his tail and bark. And he would think, "Here comes my new playmate."

At last a car stopped. Peter and Polly's father got out—with a big black dog.

The little white dog was so excited that he wiggled and waggled all over as he ran to meet them.

But do you know what that big black dog did? He just looked down at the little dog and said in dog language, "Get out of my way, you little nuisance! I'm going to be boss here!"

After that the little white dog wasn't happy any more.

The big dog was very mean to him. Not when Peter and Polly were there, of course. He pretended to be friendly then. But the rest of the time he was awful.

He wouldn't play.

He took naps on the little dog's cushion, because he liked it better than his own.

Worst of all, he was so greedy that he gobbled down his own food and half of the little dog's food too. And he dug up all the little dog's best bones!

The big dog grew bigger and fatter.

The little dog grew littler and thinner. His dishmop tail stopped waggle-waggling. His bark wasn't a woofy, happy bark now.

Peter and Polly put more and more good food in his supper dish. But most of the time the little dog didn't dare eat it because the big dog growled at him, "Leave some for me, or you know what I'll do when I get you alone!"

So the big dog would eat and eat. Then he would take a nap. Then he would walk proudly out to guard the chicken house.

But one night something different happened.

5

Peter and Polly had given the dogs an extra special supper. The big dog gobbled his down. Then, the minute the children went back into the house, he pushed the little dog away and gobbled all that supper, too.

Every bit of it—except for one small bone!

Then the big dog stretched out for a nap—with his feet on the little dog's cushion, and the rest of him on his own.

The little dog took the one small bone and gnawed and gnawed on it.

He heard Peter and Polly go to bed upstairs.

He saw the stars begin to shine.

And still the big dog slept.

The little dog tried to sleep, too. But he couldn't because he was hungry.

It got later and later.

And then do you know what happened?

There was a sound out in the chicken house! A chicken squawked!

Quick as a flash the little dog ran down the porch steps. He flew faster than a butterfly or a grasshopper straight to the chicken yard.

He barked so loudly that he sounded almost like a lion!

Peter and Polly heard the barking. They came

running downstairs and outdoors. So did their father and mother.

They all saw the lazy black dog just beginning to wake up on his own and the little dog's cushions.

They saw the old thief fox running away as if a whole pack of lions were chasing him.

And they saw the little dog come proudly out of the chicken yard.

My, how they praised that little dog! They took him into the kitchen and fed him a wonderful supper. They wouldn't even let the greedy, lazy, big dog in. He stood on the other side of the screen door, growling.

And next day they took the big dog back to the kennel where they had bought him.

And the little white dog was the watch dog. But he didn't have to do much watching because he had scared the old fox away so that he never came back.

And ever after that the little white dog had his own food and his own special cushion. And his shiny brown eyes laughed, and his dish-mop tail waggled. And his bark was a woof-y, happy one.

THE HAPPY HEN

by HELEN *and* ALF EVERS

Here is a happy brown hen.

She hasn't any teeth like the dog,
Or hands like the farmer,
Or whiskers like the cat.
And yet she is happy.
She doesn't want to moo like the cow,
Or to swim like the ducks.
She is just a happy stay-at-home hen.
But the *other* chickens wanted to travel.
So one day when their gate blew open
They rushed and scrambled and flew away.

9

But the little brown hen was too happy at home to go traveling.

Then everyone said, "Look at the brown hen.

"*She* is staying at home. She didn't want to go away with the rest. She must be ill! Perhaps she has a headache or a cold or a fever."

So the farmer put the hen to bed, near the stove.

He gave her pink pills, white pills and brown pills.

He mixed the poor hen a hot mustard plaster.

His wife made her gargle, the baby gave her rhubarb and soda, they wrapped her in blankets, with a hot-water bottle until her head drooped, and her eyes half-closed.

And she ached *all over!*

So the farmer said, "There's no hope!" and he put the hen back in the chicken yard.

Then she ran and jumped, she clucked and cackled.

She looked healthier and happier than ever.

And everyone said, "We've cured her!"

But she knew why she was healthy and happy—

Nobody bothered her and she was *home!*

FU LEE'S CRICKET

by RHODA W. BACMEISTER

Far away in a country called China, there lived a little boy named Fu Lee. He was just about as big as you are, and he liked just about the same things that you do.

He liked to climb and swing. He liked to play with the other children. He liked to eat, especially melons, and he loved to watch all the little beetles and spiders and frogs he could find. But best of all he loved his own, dear father, Fu Wong, who played with him and told him stories and sometimes brought him presents.

One day Fu Wong brought Fu Lee a present in a little square box not much wider than your hand.

"Oh! What can it be?" cried Fu Lee.

Fu Wong opened his eyes very wide and smiled. "It's alive!" he said.

Fu Lee was very much surprised.

"How can there be room for something alive in such a tiny box?" he asked.

Fu Wong laughed. "He's in there," he said, "and even his whole *house* is in there! Open it and see."

12

So Fu Lee opened the box very carefully and took out a dear little cage made of the tiniest sticks. It had a ring fastened to the top so that he could carry it around or hang it up, and inside was a fine black cricket!

Fu Lee looked at the cricket and smiled, and the cricket looked at Fu Lee and wiggled the long black antennae on his head. That is the way they said "Hello" to each other.

"I shall name him Ki-ki," said Fu Lee.

Fu Lee carried the cricket around with him that morning, and at dinner time the little cage was set not far away. Fu Lee had melon for dinner and he gave the cricket a little piece. Ki-ki liked it almost as much as Fu Lee did. Then it was time for Fu Lee to go to sleep.

"I want to take my Ki-ki," he said.

Fu Wong laughed. "People don't take crickets to sleep with them," he said, "but you may have him in your room, if you like. It is cool there, and perhaps if we made it dark he would sing you to sleep."

So when Fu Lee went to his room, Ki-ki's cage stood nearby and they laid a black cloth over it to make it dark inside. Crickets like cool, dark, quiet places.

Fu Lee lay very still and soon he heard his cricket singing, "Crick, crick, crick." It was a nice, drowsy, little noise and he went to sleep listening to it. He slept a long time, but when he woke up Ki-ki was still singing, "Crick, crick, crick."

Fu Lee wanted to see. He lifted up the cloth. But then it was bright daylight in the cage and the cricket stopped singing.

"Oh dear," said Fu Lee, "I wanted to see him open his little mouth and sing."

"You couldn't see that," Fu Wong told him, "because he doesn't sing with his mouth. He just rubs one wing against a rough place on the other to make that 'crick.' Crickets sing with their wings!"

14

That seemed very queer to Fu Lee, but in the afternoon, when it began to get a little dark, the cricket started singing again. "Crick, crick, crick," he went. Fu Lee came up softly beside the cage and watched. Ki-ki lifted his wings and rubbed them along each other. "Crick" came the sound, loud and clear. It seemed very strange that such a little fellow could make so loud a sound.

"Crick, crick, crick, crick" he went, on and on. He never seemed to get tired of making his pretty song, and Fu Lee and Fu Wong never tired of hearing him sing, either.

A GARAGE FOR GABRIEL

by CATHERINE WOOLLEY

There was once a little car whose name was Gabriel.

Now poor Gabriel had no garage. He lived outdoors in a lot where they sold used cars. He wore a sign that said, "FOR SALE—CHEAP."

There were dents in his fenders. His paint was rusty. His doors sagged.

Every day Gabriel watched the shiny new cars roll by. But they never even looked at Gabriel.

"Oh," thought Gabriel, "how I should like to go whizzing right along. How I wish I were new and shiny!"

"But, specially," he thought sadly, "how I, *how* I wish I could have a garage!"

Well, one day two ladies came along.

They said to the man who sold cars, "Have you a small car?"

He pointed to Gabriel.

"We'll try it," they said. In they climbed.

"Now!" whispered Gabriel in great excitement. "I'll show them I can whiz right along. Then the ladies will buy me and give me a garage."

"*Whiz, whiz, whiz*," went Gabriel around the block.

He was feeling mighty happy.

Round and round and round the block. *Whiz, whiz, whiz!*

"That will show them," he thought.

But the ladies cried, "Mercy, we don't want this car. It won't slow down at all."

Gabriel felt very sad.

Next day a college boy came.

"Here's a fine car," said the man.

"I'll try it," said the college boy.

"Oh, ho!" thought Gabriel. "This time I'll go very slowly, if that's what they want. Then the college boy will buy me and give me a garage."

So he went v-e-r-y, v—e—r—y, v——e——r——y, s———l———o———w———l———y.

But the college boy said, "That car's too slow!"

And off he marched.

Gabriel felt very sad.

But the next day a young lady came.

This time Gabriel was determined to do the right thing.

"I won't go too fast and I won't go too slow," he said. "But I'll show her I've got pep in my engine. Then she'll buy me and give me a garage."

17

The young lady started the engine.

"BANG!" shouted Gabriel. "BANG, BING, BANG, POP, POP!"

"My goodness!" cried the young lady. "This car's much too noisy!"

And off she hurried.

"Oh, dear!" cried poor Gabriel. "Won't *any-one* ever buy me and give me a garage? I'll never be so noisy again!"

So the next day when a man came and pressed the starter, Gabriel didn't make any noise. Not *any* noise.

"This car won't even start," said the man. He turned on his heel and left.

Well, Gabriel felt just awful. Now he was sure that he never would have a garage.

And then Jimmy and Jimmy's daddy came along.

"Have you a car for $50?" asked Jimmy's daddy.

The man was so *mad* at Gabriel, he said, "Yes —*there's* a car for $50."

"Sold!" cried Jimmy's daddy.

They climbed right in.

Gabriel was so surprised that he never had time to show off. He just acted natural.

They drove up the street and stopped in front of a little yellow house.

Then Jimmy's daddy greased Gabriel's engine till it purred like a pussycat.

"I sound real quiet!" thought Gabriel.

Then Jimmy's daddy hammered out the dents in the fenders, and oiled the hinges and fixed the sagging doors.

"I feel real good!" whispered Gabriel.

And last of all, Jimmy's daddy gave Gabriel a coat of shiny red paint.

"I look FINE!" shouted Gabriel.

Then Jimmy and his daddy and mommy and Pooch, their cat, all went for a ride.

Every time they whizzed by another car, Gabriel

19

bowed and smiled and the other cars bowed and smiled, too.

And when they came home, they whizzed right up the driveway into a little, yellow garage!

SILLY BILLY, THE FUNNY BUNNY

by CORINNA MARSH

Bobby is a little boy four years old. He has a Mommy and a Daddy and a little baby sister, Nancy.

And Bobby has lots of toys. He has a pail and shovel and a red wagon and a big box of blocks and a woolly dog and a scooter. But the toy he loves the most is his funny bunny whose name is Silly Billy.

Silly Billy is a big, soft, white, furry bunny with long pink ears. One of Silly Billy's ears stands up straight, but the other droops down over one eye. It makes him look very funny and silly. That is why he is called Silly Billy.

Bobby loves to take Silly Billy to bed with him and talk to him at bedtime.

"He talks to *me* too," Bobby said to his Mommy one night.

"*I* never heard him say anything," said Mommy.

And Daddy said, "*I* never heard him say anything."

And little Nancy just gurgled and played with her rag doll because she was only a baby and couldn't talk words yet. But *she* never heard Silly Billy say anything either.

"He doesn't talk to other people," Bobby explained. "And he doesn't talk in the daytime. He only talks to me at night in bed."

"What does he say?" asked Mommy.

"He tells me I'm a good boy," said Bobby, "and he tells me funny things."

That night Bobby took Silly Billy to bed with him as he did every night.

"Am I a good boy?" Bobby asked the bunny.

Silly Billy looked at Bobby with his funny-looking eye, and Bobby was sure he heard him say, "Yes, you are a very good boy."

"Tell me something funny now," said Bobby.

And he was sure he heard Silly Billy say, "Bibby Babby Bobby, Riding on his Hobby."

Bobby laughed and said, "Tell me some more funny things."

And he heard Silly Billy say, "Minny Manny Munny, Finny Fanny Funny."

And Bobby laughed and said, "Tell me some more funny things."

And this time he heard Silly Billy say, "Keepy Teepy Sheepy, Time to go to Sleepy."

Bobby laughed again, but it was a sleepy laugh this time. He hugged Silly Billy tight, and soon they were both fast asleep.

The next morning, when Bobby woke up, Silly Billy was right there in bed looking just as funny as ever with one ear drooping over one eye. But it was daytime and Bobby's Mommy was standing by his bed smiling. And of course Silly Billy didn't say anything.

Bobby washed his hands and face and brushed his teeth and helped put on his socks and shoes and overalls. When he was all dressed, Daddy came in with a big smile on his face. "I have a surprise for Bobby," he said.

Daddy took Bobby's hand, and Mommy came along too, and they all went out into the yard to

see the surprise. There, on the grass, was a big wooden box with a wire fence in front of it, and in the box was a real live bunny nibbling a lettuce leaf. He looked just exactly like Silly Billy—white fur, pink drooping ear, funny eye, and all—but he wasn't a toy. He was alive, and his name was Pinky.

Bobby was very happy to have Pinky, and he fed him lettuce and carrots and played with him all day long—that day and every day.

But he still takes Silly Billy to bed with him at night, and they talk together after the lights are out.

And Silly Billy says funny things to Bobby. And Bobby laughs and goes to sleep holding Silly Billy very tight in his arms.

CHRISTMAS STOCKING

by DOROTHY W. BARUCH

On Christmas eve, after Bobby Joe had un-
dressed and put on his pajamas, and after he had
brushed his teeth, do you know what he did?

He hung up his Christmas stocking.

His stocking was empty. His stocking was
flat. That's the way it was when he hung it up.

Bobby Joe looked at his Christmas stocking,
and then he climbed into bed and laid his head
down and shut his eyes—oh so tightly—and went
fast, fast, asleep.

Next morning Bobby Joe woke up. He opened
his eyes wide and he sat up in bed. There was
his stocking.

But it wasn't flat any more and it wasn't empty
any more. It was all big and round and bumpy—
full.

Bobby Joe put his hand into his Christmas
stocking. What do you think he pulled out?
Something with black and white fur and eyes and
ears and a nose and mouth and legs and feet.

It was a . . . TEDDY BEAR!

Bobby Joe put his hand into his Christmas stocking again and he pulled out something else. It was round and it could bounce, bounce, bounce.

It was a . . .

 BALL!

Bobby Joe put his hand into his Christmas stocking again and he pulled out something else. It was something in a box. It was something that would make colored marks—up and down, and 'round and 'round on paper—red, blue, green, yellow.

It was a . . .

 BOX OF CRAYONS!

Bobby Joe put his hand into his Christmas stocking again and he pulled out something else. It was a thing he could put up to his mouth and make it go *toot, toot, toot.*

It was a . . .

 HORN!

And then Bobby Joe put his hand way in, right down to the toe of his Christmas stocking and he pulled out the very last thing. It had wheels and a smokestack and a bell.

And it was a . . .

LITTLE TRAIN!

Bobby Joe reached into his stocking ONCE more, just to make sure. Yes, he had everything. Then he tiptoed into his mummy's and daddy's room and shouted something. Do you know what he shouted?

It was . . .

MERRY CHRISTMAS!

LITTLE CHICKEN

by MARGARET WISE BROWN

Once there was a little chicken who belonged
to a Rabbit.

The Rabbit found him one day just breaking
out of an egg, so he belonged to the Rabbit.

And he went where the Rabbit went.

When the Rabbit went for a walk, the little
chicken went for a walk.

When the Rabbit went into his hole to sleep
the little chicken went with him, and curled up
in the Rabbit's warm white fur.

When the Rabbit ate big wet cabbages the little chicken drank a drop of water from a wet cabbage leaf. The little chicken didn't eat cabbages. Cabbages are too big.

He liked bugs and worms.

Worms and bugs and bugs and worms—and seeds.

He went hopping about after them, and when he caught them he ate them up.

Then one day the Rabbit wanted to run—the way Rabbits run, on and on, for miles and miles.

So he said to the little chicken, "Hop along and find someone to play with while I go running around.

"But don't forget to come home to me before the sun goes down."

At first the little chicken was shy.

"Who wants to play with a little chicken?" he said.

"Besides, I don't know anyone but you."

"Plenty of creatures want to play with a little chicken," said the Rabbit.

And he kicked up his hind legs and off he ran over the hill.

There was the little chicken alone in a very big world.

Along came flying a lady bug.

Would a lady bug want to play with a little
chicken?

No indeed! Chickens eat bugs.

Then creepy crawly creepy crawly along came
a furry fat caterpillar.

Would a furry fat caterpillar want to play with
a little chicken?

No indeed! Chickens eat caterpillars.

Along came five fat sparrows.

Would they want to play with a little chicken?

Yes, they did. They were all birds.

Then came a little beaver,
A very little beaver who had just built a dam.

Would he want to play with a little chicken?

Not very much. He only liked to play with water and with streams and dams.

The little chicken marched down the road till he came to a daisy field. He stopped to look at a daisy, a white one. He was getting a little lonesome. Then softly flutter flutter flitter flutter, along came a big pink butterfly with a black nose.

Would a big pink butterfly with a black nose want to play with a little chicken?

No!

The butterfly only played with flowers and with things up in the air.

The little chicken was sitting in the dust of the road watching a shadow, when down the road, slowly, came a tired old workman.

Would a tired old workman want to play with a little chicken?

Of course he wouldn't.

And then what do you think came along?

A great big round animal covered with long sharp prickle quills.

What could it be?

A porcupine!

But the little chicken didn't want to play with him.

He was too prickly.

Then came a grizzly bear.

WOOF!
Would he want to play with a little chicken?
Not in this world.
Along came a silly little duck.

Would a silly little duck want to play with a
little chicken?

They were just the same size, the little duck
and the little chicken.

But the chicken couldn't swim.

33

Along came a gentle little monkey.

Would he want to play with a little chicken?

Of course he would. He was full of monkey shines.

And he played with the little chicken all afternoon.

But the little chicken had not forgotten what the Rabbit had said.

And just as the sun went down, he hopped on home to the Rabbit.

And the Rabbit ran home to the little chicken.

"Did you meet anyone who wanted to play with a little chicken?" asked the Rabbit.

"Some who did and some who didn't," said the little chicken.

And he curled up in the Rabbit's warm white fur and dreamed a little chicken dream.

WHO HAS SEEN THE WIND?

by CHRISTINA ROSSETTI

Who has seen the wind?
  Neither I nor you;
But when the leaves hang trembling
  The wind is passing through.

Who has seen the wind?
  Neither you nor I;
But when the trees bow down their heads
  The wind is passing by.

35

THE LITTLE WEATHER STORY

by MARGARET WISE BROWN

Snow falls down
And covers the ground
  And where is the boy who is walking?

The sun shines hot
On a sunny spot
  And where is the boy who is walking?

The rain falls down out of the sky
On the barn, on the field, on the old pig sty
  And where is the boy who is walking?

The wind blows cold across the hill
And slaps the golden daffodil
  And where is the boy who is walking?

Fog drifts in from over the sea
Gray and soft and quietly
  And where is the boy who is walking?

The sunset reddens the evening sky
Redding the barn and the old pig sty
  And where is the boy who is walking?

The night comes softly all around
Dark in the sky and dark on the ground
   And *here* is the boy who is walking.

A PICNIC ON THE HILL

by MIRIAM CLARK POTTER

One June morning Mrs. Goose baked a batch
of lovely cookies with raisins in them. When she
had finished she sat on her little porch, with her
apron on, and saw what a shining day it was. "I
believe I'll take a walk over to Old Lady Owl's
house," she thought. "I'll go the long way, on
the path through the woods. Old Lady Owl just
loves cookies, and I'll carry six to her in my basket,
for I promised that when I baked I'd take her some."

38

So she put on her floppy summer hat and started along, full of friendly feelings, with the basket over her wing.

She walked up Animaltown Avenue, saying, "How do you do?" to her friends, whether they saw her or not. Soon she came to the little path that led through the Wild Woods. It was flecked with sun and shadow. She was very glad that she had chosen to go the long way, this beautiful afternoon.

After a while she began to feel quite hungry. She thought of the cookies in her basket.

"But it would never do to eat one of them, when they are a present for Old Lady Owl," she told herself. "That is, unless I can think of a very good reason." She walked, and thought, and felt hungry, and after a while she said to herself; "I *have* thought of a very good reason. I will eat one of them because there are so many. Even with that one gobbled up, there will still be five."

So Mrs. Goose munched the cooky happily. It was really delicious. Mr. Pig had given her the recipe, and his Aunt Pink (who was a wonderful cook) had given it to him.

But after she had eaten the cooky Mrs. Goose still felt hungry.

"Well, I certainly mustn't eat another one unless I can think of a very, very good reason," she told herself. She looked into the basket, and then she thought, "Why, the reason is very clear! I ate the first one because I had so many—and I shall take the second one because, even with that gone, there will still be enough. Four is a nice number for a little present."

So Mrs. Goose ate the second cooky.

She was quite satisfied for a while. Then, after scrambling up a steep hill and resting by a little brook, she felt suddenly so hungry that she bent over and took a sniff of the four cookies still in the basket.

"I need a very, very good reason this time," she sighed to herself. But, even as she was saying it, she was beginning on a third cooky. "I'm eating this one just because I need it," she said. "I feel quite faint, really I do." She shut her eyes and munched.

Now Mrs. Goose knew perfectly well that what she had said to herself was not true, and she felt a little ashamed, really. But not ashamed enough to stop eating cookies.

"I have eaten three, I might as well have four," she told herself. "That seems reason aplenty."

After she had finished the fourth cooky, Mrs. Goose looked into her basket. She stared hard, with her bright black eyes. "Two look funny," she said. "*Very* funny! Not enough, really, for a present. I'd better eat them up, in one big gobble, so as not to seem skimpy. I couldn't take Old Lady Owl just a couple of cookies, now could I? So, here goes . . ."

She finished them up.

Then she trudged along, carrying the empty basket, and feeling a little confused and mixed-up about her plans. "But," she kept saying to herself, "I had a good reason for every cooky I ate, really I did!"

She came to Old Lady Owl's house, and her friend opened the door.

"Why, hello Mrs. Goose," she said. "Come in. Ah, you have a basket. Have you been picking berries?"

"Oh no," answered Mrs. Goose, smiling rather foolishly. "No, no, no, no!"

Old Lady Owl stared. When she heard her friend say "no" so many times she suspected that something was the matter. Then her sharp bird eyes discovered a clue.

"Why, there are some cooky crumbs on the bottom of your basket," she said. "So I guess you have been on a picnic, now haven't you?"

"Oh no," said Mrs. Goose again, opening her bill wide and cackling loud, queer laughter. "I wouldn't want to go on a picnic all alone, would I?" She just stood there, laughing and feeling foolish, wondering what to do, when all of a sudden she had an idea. "How about going on a picnic with me?" she asked. "We'll stop at my house and get the rest of the cookies. There are a lot left."

"Left—from what?" asked Old Lady Owl quickly.

"Oh—from six—" said Mrs. Goose, not explaining, and hurrying on with her talking, because she was afraid she had put her foot in it. "Come home with me—we'll find those cookies—and go up on the hill behind my house. It's such a lovely June day!" And Mrs. Goose laughed very, very loud indeed, just as though a lovely June day were funny.

Old Lady Owl gave her a quick, wide-eyed look. "There is something queer about this," she thought. But she rather liked the idea of a sudden picnic. Those crumbs in the basket had looked buttery and sugary and good. Mrs. Goose did make wonderful cookies! "Why yes, I think I'll come," said Old Lady Owl.

She blinked her eyes three times, shut her door,

and they walked away, carrying the basket between them.

Soon they came to Mrs. Goose's funny little house on Feather Lane. There they put cookies into the basket (about a dozen) and filled a pitcher with cold tea. They climbed the hill, and sat down on the fresh green grass among the delightful daisies.

"What delicious-looking cookies these are," said Old Lady Owl, when Mrs. Goose passed them. She took one and held it, waiting for Mrs. Goose to have one, too.

But after a little while she noticed that her friend was just sitting there, looking quite miserable.

"Why, aren't you going to have a cooky?" she asked.

Mrs. Goose gulped. "Thank you," she said. "I don't believe I care for any."

"But why not?"

"Oh, I just don't feel very hungry." Mrs. Goose shifted herself nervously. "I seem quite full—really I do . . ."

"But I can't understand." Old Lady Owl took another cooky. "You say 'Let's go on a picnic'. . . and then you won't eat!"

"I'll leave the eating to you," said Mrs. Goose, laughing in a queer, shaky way. "But I'll drink." And she poured out cold tea for her guest, and some for herself.

Old Lady Owl ate four cookies. "Well," she said, "this has been very pleasant. And I am glad to see that you still have a good many cookies left in the basket."

"You must take them home with you," beamed Mrs. Goose. "Here, I'll wrap them up in this paper napkin."

"How generous you are," said Old Lady Owl. "I believe you would give me *all* your cookies."

"Oh, not all of them!" Mrs. Goose laughed shaky laughter again. But she didn't explain; and

45

Old Lady Owl went home feeling that it had been, on the whole, a rather funny picnic.

"There was something the matter with her," she told herself. "I don't know what!" Then she happened to think of those crumbs in the basket. "I wonder," she said to herself, "if she was bringing me some—and then—" She laughed, a little. "It would be just like her, and she did say she felt quite full."

Of course she had thought it all out for herself. But then, Old Lady Owl was a very wise bird.

THE NEW HOUSE

by IRMA SIMONTON BLACK

Daddy and Mommy had found a nice new house, and all the family was going to move. But Bobby did not want to move. He liked his old house very much.

He liked his living room with the piano and the bookshelves and the ivy on top of them. He liked the gay red and blue striped curtains. Best of all he liked the big fish bowl that stood on a table by the window.

He liked his Daddy's and Mommy's room where the cuckoo clock hung on the wall, over the big chest of drawers. And he liked to bounce on the great big bed before it was made up all smooth. He liked to open the closet and try on Daddy's big shoes.

Bobby liked his old bathroom. He liked to play with toy boats in the tub, and to wash his hands in the little basin.

Bobby liked the kitchen in his old house. He liked to smell bacon cooking on the stove. He liked to open the little icebox door and get out his own bottle of milk.

Most of all he liked his own room. There were his shelves with his blocks and his cars and his toy people. There was his closet with all his clothes and his new warm green and red snowsuit. And best of all he loved Sancho Panza—his big red horse with the black tail and black eyes. Sancho Panza always slept at the foot of Bobby's bed.

No house could be as good as this house, Bobby thought. Bobby did not want to move at all.

But Mommy and Daddy had decided to move. Early one morning three jolly moving men came and piled all the furniture on a big truck. Bobby helped. He carried a box with his toy cars and his toy people out to the truck. Then he carried Sancho Panza and put him in the most comfort-

able place on the truck! And now all the old rooms were empty. Mommy was brushing up the kitchen floor and Daddy was taking down some curtains.

Then off went the moving men. And off went Bobby to nursery school.

When it was time to go home from school, Bobby's Mommy came for him. She took him a different way, to a different street. It was a nice street with trees on it. Bobby couldn't help himself. He liked the new street. "Which house do you like best?" asked Mommy.

"That one," said Bobby pointing to a red brick house with a little white door. And sure enough, that was Bobby's new house. And Bobby couldn't help himself this time either. He liked the house —from the outside.

Bobby reached up and rang the doorbell just for fun. Then his Mommy opened the door and they walked into the house.

Bobby went into a big room. There was his piano and there were the bookshelves and the ivy plants. Bobby knew that this must be his new living room. But where was the gold-fish bowl that stood on the table near the window?

Bobby did not know, so he went into the next room. That was a new kind of room that they

49

had not had before. It had a new big table and four chairs around the table. There was a cupboard in the corner with blue and yellow dishes on it. And there, under the window, was the goldfish bowl! Bobby ran to look at it. Then he sat up on one of the chairs. "Here is where I will eat my supper," he said.

Next Bobby ran into a shining white room. It had a white sink and a white stove and a big white icebox. It didn't look a bit like the old kitchen, but Bobby knew that it must be the new kitchen. And Bobby's mother gave him some white milk out of the new white icebox.

"This is a nice kitchen," Bobby said.

Bobby liked looking all over his new house. He ran into another room. There was the same big bed he liked to bounce. There was the big chest of drawers. There were some of Daddy's big shoes on the floor. "This is Mommy's and Daddy's room!" Bobby said. But where was the little cuckoo clock that Bobby liked? He looked and looked but he didn't find it.

Bobby went out of his Mommy's and Daddy's room. Right next to it was the new bathroom, and it wasn't at all like the old one! There was a big low tub and a big low basin and a shining low toilet. "I want to sail my boats in this tub, Mommy!" Bobby said. "It's as big as the ocean!"

His mother laughed and said, "All right, Bobby, hop into your ocean!"

But Bobby had not finished looking at his new house. He went into another room next to the bathroom. There were Bobby's own bed and his own chest of drawers. There was a clean new closet. Bobby peeked in and saw his new red and green snowsuit. But where were his shelves with his blocks and his toy people? And where was Sancho Panza? Bobby hunted and hunted but he couldn't find Sancho Panza. Had the moving men taken him? Had he jumped out of the truck? No matter how nice the new house might be, it could never please Bobby without Sancho Panza.

Bobby was worried. "Mommy, Mommy!" he called. "I need Sancho Panza!"

His Mommy was not at all worried. She laughed. "What is that across your room, Bobby?" she asked, and she pointed to something. "That's only a door," said Bobby.

"Why don't you open it?" Bobby's Mommy asked. So Bobby opened the little door and he saw . . . many, many stairs. "Stairs!" said Bobby, surprised. "But where is Sancho Panza?"

51

"Go on up," his Mommy said.

"You come too," said Bobby. They both went up the stairs. There at the top they found a big, wonderful, sunny playroom. There were all the toys that Bobby liked best. There were all his blocks and his cars and his toy people. And on one wall hung the little cuckoo clock! But that wasn't all. Over in the corner on a little bed was Sancho Panza.

"Oh!" said Bobby, hugging Sancho Panza. "This is much much better than the old house, because it has a big room for Sancho Panza and me to play in! Sancho Panza likes it better too!"

OVER IN THE MEADOW

AN OLD NURSERY SONG

Over in the meadow in the sand in the sun
  Lived an old mother turtle and her little turtle
    one
    Dig said the mother *We dig* said the one
      So they dug all day in the sand in the sun.

Over in the meadow where the stream runs blue
  Lived an old mother fish and her little fishes two
    Swim said the mother *We swim* said the two
      So they swam all day where the stream runs
      blue.

Over in the meadow in a hole in a tree
    Lived an old mother owl and her little owls three
        Tu-whoo said the mother *Tu-whoo* said the
            three
          So they tu-whooed all day in a hole in a
            tree.

Over in the meadow by the old barn door
    Lived an old mother rat and her little ratties four
        Gnaw said the mother *We gnaw* said the four
          So they gnawed all day by the old barn
            door.

Over in the meadow in a snug beehive
   Lived an old mother bee and her little bees five
     Buzz said the mother *We buzz* said the five
     So they buzzed all day in a snug beehive.

Over in the meadow in a nest built of sticks
   Lived an old mother crow and her little crows
      six
     Caw said the mother *We caw* said the six
     So they cawed all day in a nest built of
     sticks.

Over in the meadow where the grass grows so even
Lived an old mother frog and her little froggies
seven
Jump said the mother *We jump* said the seven
So they jumped all day where the grass
grows so even.

Over in the meadow by the old mossy gate
Lived an old mother lizard and her little lizards
eight
Bask said the mother *We bask* said the eight
So they basked all day by the old mossy
gate.

Over in the meadow by the old scotch pine
Lived an old mother duck and her little ducks
nine
Quack said the mother *We quack* said the nine
So they quacked all day by the old scotch
pine.

Over in the meadow in a cozy wee den
Lived an old mother beaver and her little beavers
ten
Beave said the mother *We beave* said the ten
So they beaved all day in a cozy wee den.

THE BEAR WHO WANTED TO BE A BIRD

by ADELE and CATEAU DE LEEUW

There was once a little black bear who wanted to be a bird. He wished it so hard, and thought about it so much, that finally he decided he *was* one.

Going through the forest one day he saw some birds high up in a tree. "Hello," he said. "I'm a bird, too."

The birds laughed at him. "*You're* not a bird," they said. "Birds have beaks."

The little black bear scurried through the forest until he found a thin piece of wood that had a point. He tied it to his muzzle and hurried back to the tree where the birds sat. "See," he cried, looking up, "I have a beak!"

"Just the same," they said, "you're not a bird. Birds have feathers."

So the little black bear ran as fast as he could out of the forest and found a chicken yard. There were lots of feathers lying on the ground. He picked them up and went back to the forest. There he sat down on some pine needles and stuck the feathers all over his head and his shoulders and down his front legs. Then he went to the tree where the birds sat and cried happily, "I have feathers, too. See, I'm a bird."

But the birds only laughed at him. "You're not a bird," they said. "Don't you know that birds sing?"

The little black bear felt sad, but not for long. He remembered that deep in the forest was a house where a singing teacher lived. He went there and knocked on the door. "Please teach me to sing," he begged. "I *must* learn to sing."

"It's most unusual," said the singing teacher, "but I will try. I have a wonderful system. Come in. Open your mouth. Now follow me—*do, re, mi, re, do . . . do, re, mi, re, do.*"

The little black bear practiced and practiced and practiced for a whole week, and then, feeling that he was very good indeed, he hurried back to the tree where the birds were.

"Listen," he cried. "I can sing, too." And he opened his mouth very wide, and in a deep voice sang, "*Do, re, mi, re, do . . . do, re, mi, re, do.*"

The birds laughed harder than ever. "You're not a bird," they told him. "Birds fly."

The little black bear said, "I can fly, too." He lifted first one foot, all covered with feathers, and then the other, and then hopped up and down, lifting both together. But he did not fly.

"I must get higher off the ground," he said. "Watch me." So he went to a big rock near by and climbed up on it, and looked over the edge. The ground seemed very far away. "But," he thought, "maybe if I take a running start, and don't look down, it will be all right." So he backed off, closed his eyes, ran as fast as he could to the edge of the rock, lifted his feet, flapped them—and fell, with a loud smack, on his little behind on the ground.

He opened his eyes, and felt the tears coming.

It hurt where he had fallen. His beak had slipped off; feathers were lying all over the ground.

The little birds laughed and laughed, high up in the tree, and then they all flew away together.

"You're not a bird," they called, and it floated back to him on the wind. "You're not a bird, you're a bear."

He picked himself up and walked slowly through the forest. He felt very bad, and everything ached.

He rubbed his muzzle, and was glad that the clumsy beak wasn't tied to it any more. He picked the rest of the feathers off himself, and his fur felt soft and furry. He found a bush with some beautiful red berries on it. They looked good, and he went over and stripped some off and ate them. They were delicious—much, much nicer than the worms that birds had to eat—and he ran his tongue around his black muzzle and pulled off another bunch.

After a while he met another bear, just about his size, coming toward him in the forest. "Hello," said the other bear.

"Wuf, wuf," said the little black bear. And he thought, "I like the sound of that. It's much better than having to sing *do, re, mi, re, do* in a deep voice."

"Come and see what *I've* found," his new friend said.

He led him to a big tree and climbed it. "Follow me," he said, and the little black bear did. Up in the first crotch was a bee's nest and a big comb of honey.

"Oh," said the little black bear, "what a wonderful find!" He dipped his paw in the honeycomb and licked it. Then he dipped it in again and licked it once more.

"I'm *glad* I'm a bear," he said. "Who would want to be a bird, anyhow?"

THE BLOWAWAY HAT

by LEONE ADELSON

Mother and Daddy and David were getting ready to go out for a walk.

Mother put on her new hat with the buttercups and daisies and red roses on it.

"Do you like my new hat?" she asked.

"Very pretty," Daddy said.

David said, "It's beautiful, Mommy."

When they went out Daddy said, "Button your coat, David, it's a windy day."

"I like the wind," said David. "It blows down my neck and tickles."

"So do I like the wind," Mommy added. "It blows my clothes on the wash line and dries them quickly."

"I guess I like it too," Daddy said. "It blew the clouds away this morning so the sun could shine for us."

"Can the wind blow everything, Daddy?" David asked as he skipped along.

"Oh no," replied Daddy. "It can't blow its nose."

And everybody laughed.

Suddenly the flowers on Mommy's hat began to nod.

The roses shook their heads at the daisies. The daisies waved at the buttercups. The buttercups swayed back and forth.

The wind blew a little harder, and the flowers danced a little faster.

And FASTER! AND—

Off into the air sailed Mommy's hat!

"Oh!" cried Mommy. "Oh! Oh! Oh!"

But the wind blew and the hat flew and no one could think of a thing to do.

"Why don't you fly with me?" the hat called to David. "Look! Just spread your petals and the wind will carry you along, too."

But David didn't hear because the wind blew too hard.

"Here I go!" called the hat, turning a somersault. "I can't wait for you. Good-by."

"I'll catch it for you, Mommy," David shouted, and he ran and jumped as high as he could.

"I have it!" he cried, and he *almost* caught it, but just then the wind swept up and stole the hat away from David's fingers.

"Sail along with me, hat," sang the wind softly, "I'll spin you like a feather."

"Whee! Watch me! I'm an airplane!" shouted the hat, and it made a flip-flop in the air. "My! That was exciting! I think I'll swoop."

And down it swooped.

And up it scooped.

And suddenly it looped the loop—right under David's nose.

He grabbed at it with both hands, but the wind rushed over and stole the hat right away from David's fingers.

A delivery boy came riding by on his bicycle.

"I'll get it for you. I can ride faster than that wind," the delivery boy said, and he raced swiftly down the street after the hat with David running after him.

The wind took a deep breath and blew the hat as high as a chimney.

"How's that, my happy hat?" puffed the wind.

"Oh, whirl us and twirl us some more," begged the flowers, but just then some black smoke puffed out of the tall chimney.

"Have to blow that smoke away, blow it away," panted the wind. "Work to do, work to do," and away roared the wind.

"Oh! I'm falling! I'm falling!" wailed the hat, and into a tailspin it went, down to the sidewalk.

"Come on," shouted the delivery boy. "We've got it now!" But just as they reached the spot, WHOOSH! whistled the wind back again.

"*Whew-w-w!*" went the wind. "What about some more fun, hat? Up you go!" and it snatched the hat off the sidewalk, tossed it down the street, and blew it around the corner.

David and the delivery boy hurried after it as fast as they could go, but when they turned the corner—

There was no hat!

"Too bad," the delivery boy said sadly. "It's gone. We'd better go back."

"Oh no!" declared David. "That was my Mommy's new hat. I must find it."

In the middle of the street there was a manhole. A little sign stood beside it. It read

MEN WORKING

A policeman stood close by, watching to see that the automobiles did not roll too close to the hole.

David waited until the policeman blew his whistle, and held up his hand to stop the traffic.

Then he ran to the edge of the manhole. It looked very dark down there.

"Here now," said the policeman, "don't be getting too close to the edge."

"I just want my Mommy's hat back," said David.

The policeman laughed. "Why, there's nothing down there but Tom fixing the water pipes."

"Oh, no," replied David. "I'm sure my Mommy's hat is down there."

"Well," answered the policeman, "we'll ask Tom about that. Tom! Come on up."

"Hey up there!" yelled the man in the manhole. "Something fell on my head. Feels like a bunch

of flowers. Stand back, everyone. I'm coming up."

In a moment David saw some daisies peep over the edge of the manhole.

Then roses and buttercups showed their head. Just below the flowers appeared Tom's surprised face.

The policeman took one look at Tom and laughed a big "HAW HAW HAW!"

A big truck driver leaned out of his red truck to look at Tom, and he laughed a deep "HO HO HO."

A lady driver leaned out of her car window to look at Tom, and she laughed a little "*Ha ha ha.*"

But David didn't laugh at Tom. He was too happy at finding Mommy's hat. He said, "Thank you, Tom, for helping me."

"That's O.K.," Tom replied. "I didn't do anything except catch the hat on my head. You found it all by yourself."

"Thank you, Mr. Policeman, for helping me catch Mommy's hat," said David.

"That's all right, son," he replied. "I didn't do anything except stop the traffic. You found it all by yourself."

David ran to the delivery boy. "I've got Mommy's hat back again. Thank you for helping me," he said.

"Don't mention it," replied the boy. "But I didn't do anything except help you run. After all, you found it all by yourself."

David ran all the way back to Mommy and Daddy. They were very proud of him. As he handed Mommy her pretty hat, the wind tiptoed back and tried to steal it away from David again.

"Silly hat," whispered the wind, tugging at the flowers. "Such a nice day for a spin. Come on. Don't stay here."

But this time David heard the wind.

"Oh no," he laughed. "I've got you tight, hat, and this time I *won't* let you go."

LADYBUG

by IRMA SIMONTON BLACK

One day Mimi found a bug in the yard. It was
a little red and black bug and it had a hard shiny
roundish body, so that it looked something like a
very tiny turtle. It didn't look at all like a biting
bug, so Mimi picked it up in her hand and the little
red and black bug crawled quickly all around her
palm. She was holding her hand like a little cup
so that the bug wouldn't fall off. Round and
round went the bug, and Mimi stood with her
hand way up near her face and her face way down
near her hand so that she could see the little bug
better.

Then some of the other children who were playing in the yard saw that Mimi was looking *hard*
at something. Henry came running, and Sally and
Joan and Bobby.

Bobby said, "What's that, Mimi?"

Mimi said, "It's a beetlebug. See, it's in my
hand."

Henry said, "My mother calls those ladybugs."

Bobby said, "Let me see it?" and he stretched
his neck and opened his eyes to look, and Sally

and Joan stretched their necks and opened their eyes to look until they were all around Mimi, crowding up. They were all very quiet, though, because they were looking so hard that they forgot all about their voices and besides, they didn't want to scare the little ladybug.

Then Sally said, "Let me hold it!"

Mimi opened her hand and flattened it so that the bug could walk right off her hand on to Sally's hand. Then Sally made the palm of *her* hand into a little hollow like a cup so that the little bug could walk around and around without falling off. All of its little feet tickled on her hand—such a tiny tickle that she had to stand very still to feel it at all! If she looked closely she could see tiny bright black dots on the forward part of the little bug.

"Those must be eyes!" Sally said.

Next the bug walked on Henry's hand and then on Joanie's hand, until it had walked on all the hands of all of the children. Then it started all over again on Mimi's.

Mimi said, "I wonder how he got here?"

Henry said, "I think he flew!"

Then they all looked a little harder at him and Sally said, "But he hasn't any wings!"

Just then the little ladybug was crawling on Sally's hand again and ALL of a sudden the smooth shiny sides of its body seemed to crack, and open, and out popped the neatest pair of gauzy wings you ever saw! That was where the little bug carried its wings—all folded up underneath its shell. Then it spread its wings and rose right up in the air out of Sally's hand and went sailing on a little wind over the fence.

Henry said, "There he goes back where he came from!"

Mimi called, "Goodbye, ladybug!"

And all of the children called "Goodbye bug!"

I WANT TO LEARN TO WHISTLE

by DOROTHY ALDIS

I want to learn to whistle.
I've always wanted to.
I fix my mouth to do it but
The whistle won't come through.

I think perhaps it's stuck and so
I try it once again.
Can people swallow whistles?
Where is my whistle then?

EVERYBODY GETS CLEAN

by MARY MCBURNEY GREEN

How does the MOTHER CAT wash her baby
    PUSSY?
She licks him up and down and she licks him
all around—and that's the way the PUSSY
gets a bath.

Does the COW have a washcloth when she washes
    baby CALF?
Her tongue is her washcloth when she washes
baby calf. She licks him up and down and
she licks him round and round—and that's the
way a CALF gets a bath.

Does the SQUIRREL have a comb to comb his
    bushy tail?
His claws are his comb when he combs his
bushy tail.

How does the DOG take a bath?
He jumps in the river or the brook or the
lake. He swims up and down and he swims
and he swims. Then out he jumps and shakes

75

himself—and that's the way the DOG gets dry, shake, shake, shake.

Does the BIRD have a bathtub?
There's a bird bath in the garden but a puddle of rain will do. He hops to the edge, ruffles up his feathers, and splashes the water on him —and that's the way the BIRD takes a bath.

Does the RACCOON wash his paws before he eats?
He washes his paws and he washes his food too. He holds his bite of dinner in his little fore paws, dips it in the water, and shakes it back and forth—and that's the way the RACCOON gets clean before he eats.

How does the ELEPHANT give himself a bath?
He dips his trunk in the pool and he sucks the water up. He throws back his trunk and he shoots the water out like the spray from a shower on his broad gray back—and that's the way the ELEPHANT takes a shower bath.

How do YOU get a bath?
Mommy turns the faucets in the shiny white tub. Hot water, cold water, mixed just right.

Then one, two, three and in you go. Scrub, scrub, scrub with the slippery white soap. Then one, two, three and out you go. Rub, rub, rub with the big bath towel—and that's the way YOU get a bath.

EGBERT LEARNS TO QUACK

by GRACE *and* OLIVE BARNETT

Egbert was a bright duck.

He could swim. He could dive in the best duck fashion. His waddle was quite as ducky as that of any grown-up duck.

But there was one thing Egbert could not do. He could not quack!

The old ducks said it was because he had been hatched in a nest of chicks. The young ducks said he was a bit stupid.

But, really, Egbert couldn't see any reason for quacking. He had all the corn he wanted. He had the clear pond where he could swim. Why should he try to quack?

One day Mrs. Dilly Duck found Egbert by the brook. He was pulling berries from a low bush.

"Egbert, you *must* learn to quack," said Mrs. Dilly. "You cannot be a proper duck without a quack. Come, now, do as I do."

Mrs. Dilly's bill opened wide. "Quack, quack, quack, quack," said she.

Egbert didn't care to learn. Mrs. Dilly's noisy quack hurt his ears.

78

He picked another fat blackberry. Then he opened his mouth wide. He really tried to quack. But the berry stuck in his throat.

"Queep, queep, queep, queep," said Egbert around the blackberry.

"That sounds like a chicken," said Mrs. Dilly. "I knew no good would come of being hatched by a hen." She waddled away, quacking indignantly.

Egbert couldn't swallow the berry in time to tell her about the mistake.

Egbert saw a big, juicy grasshopper. He jumped for it. But the grasshopper jumped first.

Egbert was always chasing grasshoppers. He had never caught one. But each one he saw *might* be the one he *would* catch.

He jumped again. So did the grasshopper. The grasshopper hopped. Egbert jumped.

At last the grasshopper hopped through a fence. Egbert tried to follow. But his foot caught in a loose wire. He tried to pull away, but the wire cut his foot. He tried to bite the wire. But it only hurt his bill.

The white kitten came by. "Why don't you mew?" said she. "I always do when I'm in trouble."

"I can't mew," said Egbert. "Only cats mew."

A lamb looked through the fence. "You should baa," said he.

"But I can't," said Egbert. "Only lambs do that. If you'd both keep still a minute," he added a bit crossly, "I might be able to think for myself.

"I know," he cried at last. "This is why all ducks must learn to quack. I'll quack."

Egbert opened his bill wide. He took a deep breath.

"Quack, quack, quack, quack," said Egbert. "Quack, quack, quack, quack."

The farmer's little girl heard him. In almost no time she had freed his foot.

Now Egbert can swim. He can dive. And his quack is louder than that of any other duck of his size.

A PRETTY LITTLE DOLL

by ERICK BERRY

Once there was a doll, a pretty little doll, who wouldn't be cuddled.

Can you believe it?

She didn't *like* to be rocked. She didn't *like* to be sung to.

She didn't even want to be a doll, a pretty little doll.

Can you believe it?

She thought, "If I could only be a bird, a bird with a red, red breast, I'd fly and fly and fly."

But a bird has to eat worms, fat worms and squirmy worms. It has to sleep in a nest high in a tree.

And a nest can be *very* crowded.

Yet still she didn't want to be a doll, a pretty little doll.

Can you believe it?

She thought, "If I could only be a flower, a flower with bright pink petals. I'd grow tall and tall in the sun."

But a flower has to grow in the rain too, in the wind and the rain.

And the rain can be *very* wet and cold.

Yet still she didn't *want* to be a doll, pretty little doll.

Can you believe it?

She thought, "If I could only be a rabbit, a rabbit with a fuzzy white tail. I'd hop and hop through the cool, long grass."

But a rabbit is scared of hawks and owls. He has to run from dogs and foxes.

Yet still she didn't *want* to be a doll, a pretty little doll.

Can you believe it?

She thought, "I'd like to be a cloud, a fleecy white cloud that turns pink at sunset. I'd float and float through the blue, blue sky."

But a cloud can sail too close to the sun. It can melt and vanish right away.

Yet still she didn't want to be a doll, a pretty little doll.

Can you believe it?

She thought, "If I could only be a mouse. A small gray mouse with whiskers and a long, long tail. I'd run around and in and out the house."

But a mouse has to be awake all night.

A mouse has to be scared of traps and careful of the cat.

Yet still she didn't want to be a doll, a pretty little doll.

Can you believe it?

She thought, "If I could only be a star, a bright, bright, twinkly star in the evening sky, and shine down on every one on earth."

But it's very cold up there where the stars are shining. And a star never sees a little girl playing in the sun.

But a doll can see a little girl. A doll can belong to a little girl.

She thought, "I think the nicest thing in the whole wide world is to be a doll, a pretty little doll. And be rocked and cuddled and sung to. I *like* to be a doll."

You can surely believe *that!*

TIMOTHY TITUS

by BLANCHE ELLIOTT

Timothy Titus Butteryjill
Had a red-roofed house at the foot of a hill,
And the hill rose up all green and brown
Like an ice-cream cone turned upside down.
And Timothy's house had a rosebush rack
And a porch at the front.
And a porch at the back.

And Timothy had no sister or brother,
But he had a house and he had a mother.

And once when the summer sun arose
Timothy woke and put on his clothes.
He tiptoed softly down the stair
But he couldn't find Mother anywhere.

He looked in the kitchen,
The cellar,
And hall,
He couldn't find Mother at all, at all.
He hurried quickly back up the stair,
Timothy's mother
Was not there.

Then away outdoors where the back door led
Tim looked in the garden, and rabbit shed,
And in the garage,
But it was bare.
And back to the kitchen. She wasn't there.

Then Timothy ran where the colts were kicking
"For maybe," he said, "she's berry picking."
He saw an arm. He surely had her.
It was just a man with an apple ladder.

Then he heard a step that he felt somehow
Would surely be Mother.
It was a cow.

He was rounding a bush when he felt a peck
Like his mother's kiss on the back of his neck,
On the back of his neck away up high,
He turned.
It was only a butterfly.

Then something moved in a billowy heap.
He hurried closer.
It was some sheep.
And Timothy searched both there and here
But Timothy's mother was nowhere near.

By this time Tim some way or other
Had lost his house along with his mother.
And on Tim ran in ziggety zags
Till his legs were scratched and his clothes were
    rags.
And Timothy Titus Butteryjill
Found himself 'way, 'way round his hill.

Then quickly, suddenly, up ahead
Tim saw his house—the roof was red—

And his front porch with the rosebush rack.
(Don't you remember, he left from the back?)

And Timothy ran, just lickety splitting.
His mother was on the front porch knitting.

THERE WAS TAMMIE!

by DOROTHY *and* MARGUERITE BRYAN

"Who is ready to go on a picnic?" Mother called, one fine morning.

It was exactly the sort of day for a surprise—a pleasant surprise, like a picnic.

"I am."

"I am."

"Bow-wow."

"I am."

Sally, Peter, Tammie and little George all ran to Mother, who was waiting beside their automobile.

Mother lifted little George onto the front seat.

"George and I will ride here," she said.

"And Fuzzy, too?" he asked.

"And Fuzzy, too," Mother agreed.

"Sally and Peter, you hop in the back. But watch out for the chocolate cake on the seat."

So Sally and Peter climbed into the rumble seat most carefully and sat one on either side of the cake.

"Now," said Mother, "have we forgotten anything? Chocolate cake, big umbrella, red striped

88

cushion and my new book. Picnic basket, thermos bottle, old fringed rug and Fuzzy. Little George, Sally, Peter—"

"And Tammie," shouted all the children together.

"Oh, no!" Mother objected. "I do not see how we can possibly fit in Tammie, too. We will have to leave him at home this time. You stay home, like a good dog, Tammie."

So, a little sadly, they all drove off for the picnic and left poor Tammie standing alone.

They had turned at the gate and started down the street when little George's hat blew off.

Mother stopped the car and waited while Peter climbed out and ran back to get it.

Sitting beside the hat and looking very pleased with himself—

THERE WAS TAMMIE!

Peter picked up the hat and ordered, *quite* firmly, "Go home, Tammie, old boy."

Tammie started home. Every few steps he turned around and looked at Peter.

Peter walked slowly back to the car, put little George's hat on his head again and climbed in beside the chocolate cake.

They drove on to the grocery store. Mother stopped the car across the street. She wanted to buy some animal crackers for little George.

"We will save some of them for Tammie," she promised as she started away to the store.

"I will save a whole elephant for Tammie," called little George.

When Mother came out with the crackers— there, wagging his tail and looking hopefully up at her,

THERE WAS TAMMIE!

Mother shook her finger at him and spoke very firmly, "You can*not* come with us. Go home, Tammie!

Tammie turned towards home.

Mother drove to the gas station at the corner.

After the service man had filled the tank of their automobile with gasoline and put air in the back tires, he came around to Mother.

"Is this your dog, Lady?" he asked. "He was on the step of your car." The man held out his arms and—

THERE WAS TAMMIE!

"Yes, thank you," Mother answered. "That is our Tammas. He is a very bad dog."

Being a Scotch dog, his real name is Tammas but Mother only calls him so when she is *very* stern.

The gas station man put Tammas down and Mother said, *very* sternly, "Go home, Tammas!"

The poor little fellow turned towards home—l-o-o-k-i-n-g back at every step.

Mother, Sally, Peter and little George drove out into the country. So many of the things that they passed made the children think of Tammie.

They passed a sparkling brook. Tammie would have loved to splash there with those three ducks who were marching down for a swim.

They passed Tammie's special dog friends, Michael and Patsy, trotting back from having fun. Tammie liked to go places, too.

They passed three saucy squirrels sitting by the roadside, their cheeks round with nuts. Tammie would have chased them quickly up a tree.

They passed a boy on a bicycle, with two dogs

running gayly along beside him. Tammie would have barked at them, if only he had been there.

And Tammie would have barked, too, at all the honking horns on the automobiles that passed by—if only *he* had come on the picnic instead of the chocolate cake!

Tammie loved to bark at honking horns.

They turned down a little lane where it was very quiet until

HONK! HONK! sounded behind them.

Then HONK! HONK! HONK! HONK! nearer and louder.

HONK! HONK!

The car passed them.

A large man was driving it and sitting beside him, looking at them out of the window—

THERE WAS TAMMIE!

The large man was Mr. Beam, their next door neighbor. "I guess that you forgot your Tammie," he said. "I found him back at the gas station. We have had a chase to catch you."

Tammas looked at Mother.

Mother looked at Tammas.

"Well," said Mother. "Here he is!"

"Well," said Mother again, "thank you, Mr. Beam. Jump in Tammie." So—

Happily, they drove on for the picnic. The chocolate cake was on the floor and tucked in between Sally and Peter on the rumble seat—

THERE
      WAS
           TAMMIE!

NEW SHOES

by IRMA SIMONTON BLACK

New shoes are slippery
Polished and trippery
I like new shoes.
I like the black ones, all aglow
From shiny heel to shiny toe.
I like the white ones, too, that feel
Velvety from toe to heel.
I like plain brown ones to play in
Go to school and spend the day in.
I like new shoes.

OLD SHOES

by IRMA SIMONTON BLACK

Old shoes are lumpy
Scratched up and bumpy
I like old shoes.
I like the way they bend and feel
Wrinkle-y from toe to heel.
I like the way no one says "No"
When I scrape them on the toe.
I wear new shoes when I go out
But old ones when I crawl about.
I like old shoes.

KATY NO-POCKET

by EMMY PAYNE

Big tears rolled down Katy Kangaroo's brown
face. Poor Katy was crying because she didn't
have a pocket like other mother kangaroos. Freddy
was Katy Kangaroo's little boy and he needed a
pocket to ride in. All grown-up kangaroos take
awfully big hops and little kangaroos, like Freddy,
get left far behind unless their mothers have nice
pockets to carry them in.

96

And poor Katy didn't have any pocket at all.

Katy Kangaroo cried just thinking about it, and Freddy cried, too.

Then, all of a sudden, Katy had a wonderful idea! It was so wonderful she jumped six feet up in the air.

The idea was this: Other animal mothers had children and they didn't have any pockets. She'd go and ask one of them how they carried their babies!

Freddy looked all around to see whom to ask and Katy looked all around to see, too. And what they both saw were two bubbles rising up from the river right beside them.

"Mrs. Crocodile!" said Katy, feeling lots better already. "*She* hasn't any pocket. Let's ask her!"

A lot of big muddy bubbles came up through the water and then Mrs. Crocodile stuck her head up and opened her *enormous* mouth and smiled.

"Why, Katy Kangaroo! What can I do for you today?"

"Please, Mrs. Crocodile, I am so sad," said Katy. "I have no pocket and Freddy has to walk wherever we go and he gets so tired. Oh dear, oh dear!"

And she started to cry again.

The crocodile began to cry, too, and then she said, "B-b-but—What—can *I* do?"

"You can tell me how to carry Freddy," said Katy. "How do you carry little Catherine Crocodile? Oh, do *please* tell me."

"Why, I carry her on my back, of course!" said Mrs. Crocodile.

She was so surprised that anyone shouldn't know that she forgot to cry any more.

Katy was pleased. She said, "Thank you," and as soon as she got to a good squatting-down place, she squatted and said, "Now, Freddy, climb on my back. After this it will be so simple—no trouble at all."

But it wasn't simple. In the first place, Freddy could not crawl up onto her back because his knees stuck out. He couldn't hang on because his front legs were too short. And when he did manage to hang on for a few minutes and Katy gave a long hop, he fell off—bump, bang—with a terrific thump.

So Katy saw that she couldn't carry her baby on her back.

Katy and Freddy sat down again and thought and thought.

"I know! I'll ask Mrs. Monkey. I'm sure she can help me."

So Katy and Freddy set off for the forest and very soon they found Mrs. Monkey. She had her young son, Jocko, with her and Katy Kangaroo hurried so to catch up with them that she was almost out of breath. But finally she managed to squeak, "Please, Mrs. Monkey, how do you carry Jocko?"

"Why, in my arms, of course," said Mrs. Monkey. "How else would any sensible animal carry anything?" And she whisked away through the trees.

"Oh dear," said Katy, and a great big tear ran across her long nose. "I can't carry anything in these short little arms, oh *dear!* She wasn't any help at all. What are we going to do?" And she just sat down and cried harder than ever.

Poor Freddy! He hated to see his mother cry, so he put his paw to his head and he thought, and thought, and *thought.*

"What about the lion?" he asked when Katy stopped crying a little.

"They don't carry their children. The poor things walk just the way you do," said Katy.

"There's—there's birds," said Freddy. "How do they carry their babies?"

"Birds!" said Katy. "The mother birds push their children out of the nest and they squawk and shriek and flap their wings about it."

Then all at once Katy Kangaroo stopped crying and looked at Freddy. "They do say that the owl knows almost everything," she said slowly.

"Well, then, for goodness' sake, let's ask *him!*" said Freddy. They found the owl asleep in an old dead tree, and he was cross because he didn't want to be waked up in the middle of the day. But when he saw that Katy was so sad he came out, blinking and ruffling his feathers and said in a scratchy voice, "Well! Well! what is it? Speak up! And speak loudly. I'm as deaf as a post."

So Katy stood under the tree and screamed at him, "I'm a mother kangaroo and I haven't a pocket to carry my child in. How shall I carry him? What shall I do?"

"Get a pocket," said the owl and went to sleep again.

"Where?" cried Katy. "Oh, please, don't go to sleep before you tell me where!"

"How should I know?" said the owl. "They sell that sort of thing in the City, I believe. Now, kindly go away and let me sleep."

"The City!" said Katy, and looked at Freddy with big, round eyes. "Of course, we'll go to the City!"

Katy was so excited that she almost left Freddy

behind as she went leaping over bushes and hopping along the path, singing in a sort of hummy
way a little song she had just made up:

"Hippity! Hoppity!
Flippity! Floppity!
Wasn't it a pity?
I didn't know
It was to the City
I should go!"

She hopped so fast that Freddy could hardly
keep up, but at last they left the woods behind
and came to the City where there were stores and
houses and automobiles.

The people all stared and stared at Katy, but
she didn't notice it. She was looking for pockets
and she saw that almost everybody had them.

And then, all at once, she saw—she could hardly
believe it—a man who seemed to be ALL pockets!
He was simply covered with pockets. Big pockets,
little pockets, medium-sized pockets—

Katy went up to him and laid a paw on his arm.
He was a little frightened, but Katy looked at him
with her soft brown eyes and said, "Please, dear,
kind man, where did you get all those pockets?"

"These pockets?" he said. "You want to know where I got all these pockets? Why, they just came with the apron, of course."

"You mean you can really get something to put on with ALL those pockets already in it?" asked Katy.

"Sure you can," said the man. "I keep my hammer and nails and tools in my pockets, but I can get another apron, so I'll give you mine."

He took off the apron and dumped it
UPSIDE DOWN
Out fell a saw, wrench, nails, a hammer, a drill, and lots of other tools. Then the man shook the apron hard and turned it right side up again and hung it around Katy's neck and tied it behind her back.

Katy was so pleased and excited and happy that she couldn't speak. She just stood still and looked down at the pockets and smiled and smiled and smiled.

By this time, a big crowd had gathered to see what Katy Kangaroo was doing.

When they saw how pleased she was, they all smiled, too.

At last Katy was able to say "Thank you" to the nice, kind man, and then what do you think she did?

She popped Freddy into a very comfortable pocket and she hippity-hopped home faster than ever before because, of course, she didn't have to wait for Freddy.

And when she got home, what do you think she did?

Well, she had so many pockets that she put Freddy into the biggest one of all. Then, into the next largest she put little Leonard Lion. Thomas Tortoise just fitted into another pocket.

Sometimes she had a baby bird if its mother was busy at a worm hunt. And there was still room for a monkey, a skunk, a rabbit, a raccoon, a lizard, a squirrel, a 'possum, a turtle, a frog, and a snail.

So now, all the animals
like Katy's pockets better than
any other pockets in the whole forest.
And Katy Kangaroo
is very happy because now
SHE HAS MORE POCKETS THAN
ANY MOTHER KANGAROO
IN THE WORLD!

GEORGIE'S BABY SISTER

by KATHLEEN L. BERNATH

Georgie has a new baby sister.
She lies in her crib all day long.
She can't talk like Georgie. She's too little.
She can't walk like Georgie. She's too little.

She makes funny noises. Sometimes she cries.
She doesn't eat anything, because she hasn't any
teeth.
She just drinks milk all the time.
She can't go to the bathroom. She's too little.
She's always wet, and someone is always chang-
ing her.

Visitors look at her and say, "Oh, isn't she
sweet?" and "Georgie, don't you *love* your little
sister?"
And Georgie doesn't say anything, because he
doesn't know her very well yet.

But he likes her when he goes over to her crib
and says "Hello," and she smiles at him without
any teeth, and waves her fat pink arms at him!

THE HOUSE OF THE MOUSE

by LUCY SPRAGUE MITCHELL

The house of the mouse
is a wee little house,
a green little house in the grass,
which big clumsy folk
may hunt and may poke
and still never see as they pass
this sweet little, neat little,
wee little, green little,
cuddle-down hide-away
house in the grass.

WHAT ABOUT WILLIE?

by LE GRAND

Once there was a big, dark, cold, rainy night and right in the middle of it was WILLIE.
Willie was cold.

Willie was wet.

Willie was hungry.

Willie was a little stray kitten who was looking for a home.

Not too far away was a little, green house beside a brook. A little boy named Tommy lived there.

Now Tommy had a home but he didn't have a kitten.

So on this rainy night, Tommy was drawing pictures of the kind of kitten he wanted most.

Just like Willie!

In a deep, dark pool in the brook, not far from the green house a big old catfish swam round and round. He didn't care at all about rain or how cold and dark the night was.

But Willie cared.

For Willie was still out in the night, going on and on, looking for a home.

Then he heard someone slip-slopping through the puddles, and a man walked past.

Willie scampered up to the man and said, "Meow." But it was old Mr. Greeble who didn't like cats at all.

"Scat," said old Mr. Greeble.

And Willie scatted.

He came to a house.

It was a bright, cheerful, white house. Willie liked it.

He thought it would be nice to live there.

Just then Mrs. Riffles came hurrying home to the white house.

Willie curved his back and raised his tail straight up in the air.

He tried to rub against Mrs. Riffles' ankles, but Mrs. Riffles didn't even know Willie was there. She opened the door and went in the house.

And so did Willie!

Willie went down the hall,

and up the stairs,

and into the bedroom,

and up on the bed.

Then he purred and stretched.

Willie was warm and dry. He fell asleep.

Mrs. Riffles came up the stairs and into the bedroom.

She turned on the light—

And then she saw Willie!

And *there* were Willie's muddy paw prints all over Mrs. Riffles' best green satin bedspread!

"Oh," shouted Mrs. Riffles. Willie opened one eye.

"Go away," shouted Mrs. Riffles. Willie opened both eyes.

"SCAT," shouted Mrs. Riffles. She got the broom and pushed Willie off the bed. She chased him out of the room, and down the stairs, and through the hall, and out the door, out into the night, the cold, rainy night.

Willie went on and on.

Then he saw another house.

Willie went to the front door and said, "Meow."

But no one came.

Willie went to the back door and said, "Meow."

But no one came.

Then Willie saw something.

Beside the house was a little, tiny house, just the right size for Willie.

There was a little door in it and Willie peeked in.

It looked dry and warm in there.

Willie crept in.

And then something went WOOF!

Willie was in the *doghouse*.

But not for long — — — — — —

Willie's fur rose until he looked as round as a ball.

He seemed to roll through the air he went away so fast.

Willie was out in the cold again.

It was still raining. Willie was still cold.

And he was still looking for a home.

There weren't any more houses for a long time.

Finally, when it was almost morning, Willie came to another house.

It was the little green house beside the brook.

Willie went all around the house and said, "Meow-Meow."

But no one came.

At last Willie crouched under a bush that grew beside a deep, dark pool in the brook.

In the pool was the big, old catfish that swam round and round.

He still didn't care at all about the rain, or about how cold and dark the night was. But he was beginning to want breakfast.

He swam round and round.

And then, he saw a worm.

The big, old catfish looked all around to see if there was anyone fishing.

And there wasn't.

There wasn't anyone there but Willie.

Gulp! the catfish swallowed the worm, and was caught on the hook of a fishing line Tommy had left in the pool.

Willie saw the fishline twitch.

Willie crouched and wiggled his tail, and sprang, and caught the fishline with his claws.

Willie pulled.

The fish pulled back.

Willie pulled harder.

So did the fish.

Willie got all tangled up in the line.

He couldn't get loose.

And then the fish pulled so hard that Willie was dragged right down to the pool.

His feet were in the water. It was cold. He was pulled farther.

The water was up to his soft, little white tummy.

It was very cold water.

Willie yowled.

He yowled so loud that he woke up Tommy.

Tommy looked out the window.

He saw Willie struggling in the water.

Tommy hurried down the stairs and put on his rubbers and rushed out the door.

He ran through the rain to the brook where Willie was crying.

Then Tommy grabbed the fish pole and pulled.

The fish pulled.

Willie pulled.

Everyone pulled.

But Tommy pulled hardest, so up came Willie and the catfish.

Willie was so frightened he ran off as fast as he could.

Tommy couldn't catch him.

So there was Tommy who wanted a kitten.

And there was Willie who wanted a home—running away from it.

"Aw!" said Tommy, "he was an orange and black and white kitten. Just what I wanted."

Willie ran down the road until he came to a fence.

He jumped up on the fence and then he saw a little box.

It was just a tiny, little box. But it was big enough for Willie to hide in. And he did.

Tommy took the fish home. It tasted very good for breakfast and Tommy ate about half of it.

But between bites he kept saying, "Aw—I nearly had a kitten—Aw!"

After breakfast Tommy went to get the mail. He was still feeling sad.

He went across the field and down the road to the crossroads where the mailbox stood. There wasn't any mail, but he saw something else. Willie was in the mailbox!

Tommy took Willie home, and warmed him and dried him, and gave him a big piece of fish.

"Because," said Tommy proudly, "Willie really caught it."

And what about Willie?

Well, every day after that Willie got plenty of milk and fish. And the little green house beside the brook which was Tommy's home was Willie's too.

Willie wasn't a stray kitten any more.

MOTHER KNEW

by HARRIET EAGER DAVIS

Snow fell so thick
  In cold December,
I couldn't remember
There was such a thing
  As Spring!
But Mother smiled,
  Said: "Funny child,
"That's Nature's trick.
  "She's often late—
  "Just wait!"

So sure enough one day the air
  Felt soft and different everywhere.
But then it sleeted and froze and blew,
  And I didn't believe my mother knew.

Till all of a sudden the buds popped out.
  And fat red robins began to shout,
And dandelions splashed in the sun
  Right where the ice-trickles used to run,
And even common old dirt smelled good!
  And Spring came here
  For another year,
Just as my mother said it would!

WHEN SUSIE WAS JUST THE RIGHT SIZE

by LOUISE WOODCOCK

Susie was a little girl who always seemed to be the wrong size. Sometimes she was too big. Sometimes she was too little. This is the kind of thing that sometimes happened.

One morning she thought she would like to take a ride in Baby Robin's gocart. She climbed in. It was a very tight squeeze.

"Susie!" called her big sister Margie. "Get right out of there! You're too big to ride in that gocart!"

Susie climbed out and looked around. She still wanted a ride. There was big brother Peter's bicycle leaning against a tree. She wheeled it out on the path. Then she tried to make it stand up while she climbed on the back step. But the front wheel wobbled and then *crash*—the bicycle fell right over with Susie in a heap on top of it.

Peter was just coming around the house. "Susie, you leave my bicycle alone!" he shouted. "You know very well you're too little to ride a bike!"

Susie crawled off the bicycle. Her chin was bumped. Her arm was scratched. Her knee was scraped. And Peter was cross at her. She began to cry.

The lady next door looked over her garden wall. "Why, Susie Sanders!" she said. "Get right up and stop crying. You're much too big to cry!"

Susie got up. She almost stopped crying. She thought she could really stop if she had one of the fresh chocolate cookies her mother had baked. She went into the house and out to the pantry. But the cookie jar was on a very high shelf. Susie pushed a chair to the shelf and climbed up on it. But still the shelf was too high.

"I'm just too little to get those cookies, that's all!" said Susie and she almost cried again.

And so it went on. She always seemed to be just too big or just too little until—one time—there came a day when Susie was JUST THE RIGHT SIZE!

It was one Saturday, when Peter and Margie didn't have to go to school. Daddy and Mother decided to have a picnic. They would all drive out to the Country House where they lived in the summer. It wouldn't be just a picnic either, for they would sleep in the house that night and not come home until the next day.

Everybody packed pajamas and toothbrushes and slippers in the big suitcase. Mother packed meatloaf and eggs and lettuce and butter and oranges and milk in a big basket. Then everybody climbed into the car and waved goodbye to the City House.

Daddy started the car and they drove and drove. First they rolled through city streets. Then they crossed a white bridge and rode past green fields. They passed some woods and some cows in a meadow. At last they came to the Country House beside a blue lake.

The children all jumped out of the car. Daddy felt in his pocket for the key to let them into the Country House. Then he looked very funny. He felt very quickly in all his pockets several times. He looked at Mother.

"I've forgotten the key!" he said.

"Oh, dear!" said Mother.

"Oh, shucks!" said Peter.

"Oh, dear!" said Margie.

"Dear—dear—dear," said Baby Robin hopping around. (He didn't really know why he said it.)

"Can't we get in at all?" asked Susie.

"Not unless we can find some window or door unlocked," said Daddy. "We may have forgot one somewhere."

He walked all around the house. He tried all the doors and he tried all the windows till just one was left, a little high window at the back of the house. That was unlocked. Daddy shoved it open.

"If someone could climb through this little pantry window, he could go through the house and open the front door," said Daddy.

"Let me climb in and open it!" cried Peter.

"No, you're too big. You couldn't get in," said Daddy.

"Oh, let me climb in! I'm smaller than Peter," Margie begged.

"You're too big too," said Mother looking at Margie and then at the window.

"Me in!" shouted Baby Robin. He could only say little words like that.

"Oh, he's too little to reach the lock," said Margie. They all knew that.

Daddy looked around at all the children. "I think I could put Susie through that window," he said.

"Yes! Yes!" cried Susie.

He held out his hand to her. "Now Susie, listen carefully. I'll put you through the pantry window. You'll find you're on the wide shelf inside. Climb down to the floor—there's the stool there to step on. Then go through the house and open the door."

"It will be a little dark because the shades are down. But you know where to go," said Mother.

Daddy picked up Susie and held her high. Mother steered her feet in backward through the window. There was just enough room for all of her to get through—her feet, her knees, her arms and shoulders. And last of all Susie pulled in her head and found she was crouched on the pantry shelf.

Near the shelf there stood a stool, as Daddy had said. Susie carefully slid her feet down to the stool, and then off to the floor.

It was rather dark in the pantry. It was darker still in the kitchen. Something big and white was standing against the wall. It looked a little like a polar bear. Then Susie remembered that polar bears live up in the north. She looked at it hard. It was only the big refrigerator after all. She felt her way along the wall until she came to the dining room door.

The dining room was even darker than the kitchen or the pantry. Susie scuffed on with little short steps so as not to bump anything. At last she came to the big front hall. Something in the corner stood tall and dark. At first it looked like an Indian. But Susie remembered that Indians didn't live here any more near the Country House. She looked at it hard. It was only Daddy's long raincoat with Peter's Indian headdress hung over it.

Then she heard Daddy's voice outside. He was at the big door across the hall.

"Open the door, Susie Girl," he said.

"Turn the lock all the way around!" shouted Peter.

Susie had to stand on her very tiptoes to reach the lock. She turned it around as hard as she could. "Erk!" said the lock. Then "Click!" it said and the door was unlocked. Daddy pushed it open very slowly so as not to bump Susie.

"Good girl, Susie!" Daddy said and gave her a pat on the top of the head.

Susie went out on the sunshiny porch. She had to blink her eyes because the sun was so bright. Mother smiled at her. Margie gave her a tap. Baby Robin hugged her around the waist as though she'd been gone for a very long time. Even big brother Peter said, "Good for you, Suze. I thought you'd be scared."

Susie followed Mother back into the house. She watched Mother push the window shades up.

At last Susie said, "Sometimes I'm just too little to do things. Sometimes I'm just too big to do things. But *this* time, Mommy, I was JUST THE RIGHT SIZE!"

THE RAIN IS RAINING

by ROBERT LOUIS STEVENSON

The rain is raining all around
    It falls on field and tree
It rains on the umbrellas here
    And on the ships at sea.

LITTLE BOBO AND HIS BLUE JACKET

by TONY BRICE

Bobo was a little elephant who lived in the green jungle. When he was *very* little he didn't wear anything at all.

But when Bobo grew a little bigger his mother made him a lovely blue jacket with two big pockets. And when Bobo put on the blue jacket he was the happiest little elephant in all the world.

He went right down to the water hole to show his blue jacket to the zebras, giraffes, and little hippos. As Bobo was strutting around, being admired by all the animals, something DREADFUL happened!

Bobo slipped on a log and fell—SPLASH—into the muddy water.

When he got up, he looked at his lovely blue

jacket. It was all covered with sticky brown mud.

The other animals laughed, but Bobo didn't. He cried!

He trotted home to his mother, crying all the way.

"Don't cry, Little Bobo," said his mother. "We'll take your blue jacket to the laundry, and have it washed until it is as good as new."

So Bobo's mother started off with the muddy blue jacket in her trunk, and Bobo trotted along beside her. Soon they came to the old monkey's laundry under the big baobab tree.

"Can you wash Little Bobo's blue jacket, quick as a wink?" asked Bobo's mother. And she showed the jacket to the old monkey.

But the old monkey was a little hard of hearing

and, besides, he was splashing so loudly in his wash-tub that he thought Bobo's mother said, "Can you wash Little Bobo's blue jacket and make it shrink?"

So the old monkey scrubbed the jacket in very soapy water, with a whole bottle of "Shrinko" in it. And when the blue jacket was washed and ironed, it was so small that the smallest elephant in the world couldn't have worn it.

When Bobo saw his blue jacket again he cried! His mother cried too!

Even the old monkey cried into his washtub, until it overflowed!

At last Bobo stopped crying and said, "If *I* can't wear my lovely blue jacket, maybe I can give it to someone who *can!*"

So he asked the little giraffe to try it on. But the blue jacket was too small for him.

The little zebra tried it on, but it was too small for *him.*

It was too small for the little lion.

It was too small for the little tiger. And it was too small for the little hippo!

Then a tear trickled down Bobo's cheek and he sobbed, "Isn't there *anyone, anywhere,* who *can* wear my lovely blue jacket with the two big pockets?"

"I hope *I* can," panted Big Brother Hippo, who had come running when he heard that Bobo wanted to give his jacket away.

"I've *always* wanted a lovely blue jacket with two big pockets."

Big Brother Hippo picked up the blue jacket and pushed and wriggled and shoved until he got one front leg in a sleeve of the jacket.

Then he pushed and wriggled and shoved some more, and pulled and struggled until he got the other front leg in the other sleeve of the jacket.

But the jacket was so very tight that Big Brother Hippo couldn't move a muscle. He would have been standing right there yet if Bobo hadn't pulled it off.

Then Bobo looked at the blue jacket. Somehow it looked bigger. It WAS bigger! Big Brother

Hippo had tried so hard to get the jacket on that he had stretched it. So Bobo tried it on himself. And it JUST EXACTLY FITTED HIM!

And Bobo was so happy to be able to wear his blue jacket with the two big pockets again—that he even wore it to bed that night!

MICHAEL AND HIS STEAM ROLLER

by INEZ BERTAIL

Michael gave three big pushes, hopped on his scooter, and rolled down the hill.

"Beep-beep! Look out of the way!" he called, going faster and faster. At the bottom of the hill, the path curved around a tree. Michael leaned sideways. The scooter curved around the tree. Then, ZING—the scooter skidded and Michael fell off in a heap.

By the time his mother reached him, Michael was sitting on the ground rubbing his knee.

"Did you hurt yourself?" his mother asked.

"No," Michael said, getting up. "But look at that old hole in the path. That's what made me fall. I wish they'd fix that old hole!"

Just then Michael heard a clanking and a rumbling behind him. He turned and saw a big steam roller coming slowly along the path into the park. It was rolling straight toward Michael, so Michael grabbed up his scooter and backed off the path. The steam roller clanked slowly to a stop right in front of the hole in the pavement. The driver stepped down.

"You going to fix the path?" Michael asked.

"Yep—if I can keep Old Mike going long enough," the man said.

"Mike? Who's that?" Michael asked.

"My old steam roller here."

"That's my name, too," said Michael.

"It is? Well, you two Mikes ought to get along fine," the man said. "But this one is kind of broken-down. We'd have been here yesterday if Old Mike hadn't sprung another leak in his boiler."

Two men drove up in a little truck. They took out their pickaxes and shovels and started to clear away the stones and broken pieces of pavement. Michael watched while his mother went inside the playground to sit on a bench and knit.

Suddenly there was a hissing noise from the steam roller. The man who drove the steam roller went over quickly, with Michael right at his heels! "Poor Old Mike! Another leak!"

"Where?" asked Michael.

"In the boiler," the man said. "This round part in the middle is the boiler. There's water in it, and a fire down below." He opened a door, and Michael saw there was a coal fire burning inside.

There was another loud hiss, and some white steam came out the door.

"See?" the man said. "There's a little hole in the bottom of the boiler. Water leaks down on the fire."

"Ssss—ssssss—sss," said Old Mike.

"Will it work now, with a leak?" Michael asked.

"Maybe, if the leak doesn't get any bigger," the man answered. "But Old Mike's boiler has been patched so many times it's *all* patches by now."

Michael understood about patches. He had them

on the knees of his overalls and trousers when they got holes in them.

And all the time the old steam roller kept saying a steady "Ssss—ssss—ssss."

By this time the two workmen had cleared away all the broken pieces of the pavement, and had shoveled tar mixed with small stones onto the path. They called to the man that everything was ready for the steam roller.

The steam-roller man climbed up into his seat and pulled a lever. Hissing and clanking, the steam roller rolled over part of the path, where the hole had been. Now it was flat and smooth and hard. Michael smiled. Now he could ride right into the playground when he raced down the hill on his scooter, he thought.

"A steam roller is a wonderful thing!" he said.

The man started the big roller backwards. It was hissing louder now, SSSSSS——SSSSSS, but it still worked. As it rolled past him, Michael saw that the piece of smooth pavement was wider.

"One more trip will do it!" the man called. He pulled the big lever. The steam roller shook a little, hissed louder, and jerked forward. SSSSSS—— SSSSSS. Suddenly there was the biggest, loudest CLANK Michael ever heard! CLANKETY-

CLANK! The long arm dropped off the side. Old Mike stopped.

"That's all!" the man said. "Piston's broken! That's the end of Old Mike."

Another man came up. "All finished here?" he asked.

"Nope," said the man, "can't finish anything with this brokendown steam roller. It's just a piece of junk!"

"I guess you're right," the other man said. "The new steam roller came in this morning just after you left. You'll have it tomorrow and we'll get rid of this old one."

Old Mike hissed, not so loud now because his fire was going out and and he knew he was finished.

But Michael liked the old steam roller, even if it was broken. He ran into the playground and found his mother. Michael was excited.

"Mommy—Mommy! The park man is going to have a new steam roller. Could I ask him for the old one? Could I, Mommy?"

Michael's mother smiled at him. But she shook her head. "Now Michael, do be sensible," she said. "Where could you keep such a big thing? There's no room in our apartment for a steam roller. Besides, it takes a man to run a machine like that,

133

someone who knows about engines and such things —like Uncle Bill."

Of course, Michael knew his mother was right. But having a steam roller would be fun—just to sit on and pretend to drive.

"Maybe Uncle Bill would like to have the steamroller, Mommy. He's good at fixing things. And he has a big truck, and a snow plough. I bet *he* could drive the steam roller!"

This time Michael's mother put down her knitting and looked quite serious. "Michael Jones! *That* is a *good* idea! Uncle Bill does so many things, he might really be able to use that steam roller. I'll go right over and speak to that steamroller man before he goes away."

Old Mike was still gently hissing. Michael's mother talked to the man. He said yes, he would sell the old steam roller to anybody that wanted to buy it.

When they got home, Michael's mother telephoned to Uncle Bill who lived in a little town across the river. Uncle Bill had a big barn where he fixed things. The big sign on his barn said:

BILL'S TINKER SHOP
IF IT'S BROKEN ⋄⋄⋄ I CAN FIX IT!

Michael heard his mother talking on the telephone to Uncle Bill. "It was Michael's idea," she said. "Of course, it's old, and right now it's broken. But I wouldn't be surprised if you could fix it."

Uncle Bill came to town the next day and went to the park with Michael. The old steam roller was there but it wasn't hissing any more. The steam-roller man was there too, with a shiny new steam roller, finishing the pavement. Uncle Bill looked at Old Mike. He talked to the steam-roller man, and they shook hands.

Michael was very excited.

"Did you buy it?" he asked.

"I sure did!" said Uncle Bill. "It's going to be fun having a steam roller. There are lots of jobs I can do with it. And, of course, it's really half yours, Michael, because you thought of it."

The next day Uncle Bill drove into the city with his tools. He worked all day on Old Mike.

At last the old steam roller was fixed. Uncle Bill drove it across the bridge over the river to his barn. Then he tried out Old Mike to see if it would work. He made a new driveway from the road to his tinker shop, and ran Old Mike over it to smooth it down. Then he telephoned to Michael, and told him the steam roller was all fixed.

"You can come out now and ride on it," he said.

Michael's mother took him to visit Uncle Bill the next day. The very first thing, he asked if he could ride on the steam roller.

"You sure can," said Uncle Bill. "But before you get up, look at this!"

He pointed to the name he had painted on the boiler of the steam roller. There in big red letters Michael saw:

MIKE

"Good Old Mike," Michael said.

"And look," Uncle Bill said, "here's a special seat I made for *you*, right beside mine."

That very afternoon Uncle Bill got a telephone call to come and roll the tennis courts in town. Soon he had Old Mike rolling down the road. And there was Michael sitting beside him, on his special seat, helping to drive the steam roller!

MUD

by POLLY CHASE BOYDEN

Mud is very nice to feel
   All squishy-squash between the toes!
I'd rather wade in wiggly mud
   Than smell a yellow rose.

Nobody else but the rosebush knows
How nice mud feels
Between the toes.

JUMP OR JIGGLE

by EVELYN BEYER

Frogs jump
Caterpillars hump

Worms wiggle
Bugs jiggle

Rabbits hop
Horses clop

Snakes slide
Seagulls glide

Mice creep
Deer leap

Puppies bounce
Kittens pounce

Lions stalk
But—
I walk!

THE VERY STYLISH FARM

by VAL TEAL

The little woman lived in a little white house on her farm. She had two noisy boys, and a mooing cow, and a barking dog, and a meowing cat, and a quacking duck, and some clucking chickens, and a little squealing, grunting pig, and a rooster that said COCK A DOODLE DOO.

Every day she listened to the pleasant sound of their voices. Every day she listened to the merry sound of their play. It sounded good to the little woman.

But one day she said, "What we need is some style. I am afraid we are very common."

So she bought the cow a lovely straw hat. It

had roses and daisies all around it. It had holes for her ears to stick through. The cow looked very stylish in her new hat.

But she could not eat hay in the hat. When she put her head down, the hat flopped over her face. So she just stood in the barn door and looked very, very stylish.

Then the little woman bought a fine leather harness for the dog. It had bright glass sets in it. It had beautiful brass buckles. The dog looked very stylish in his new harness.

But the harness bothered the dog. He could not fight the neighbor's dog with it on. So he just sat on the steps and looked very, very stylish.

Then the little woman bought a ribbon for the cat. It was a wide satin ribbon. It made a beautiful big bow back of the cat's ears. It had three little silver bells tied in the bow. The cat looked very stylish. "Meow, tinkle tinkle. Meow, tinkle tinkle. Tinkle tinkle meow," went the cat with her bells. But the cat could not catch mice with her fine new ribbon and her bells around her neck. So she lay on the porch and looked stylish.

Then the little woman made a lovely pool for the duck. It had lily pads in it. The water was clean and clear. She put the white duck in the pond. He looked very stylish in his clean lily pond. But there were no bugs to catch in the clean, clear pond. So the duck just floated on the water and looked stylish.

Then the little woman got leg bands for the hens. They had the chickens' names on them. She clamped them on the hens' legs. They looked very stylish in their pretty leg bands. But the chickens could not scratch in the dirt with their pretty leg bands on. So they just stood in a row and looked stylish.

The little woman put a leg band on the rooster, too. The rooster stood at the head of the row and looked very, very stylish.

Then the little woman bought a new trough for the pig.

She took a pail and a brush and scrubbed the pig. He was clean and shining pink. She fenced him into a grassy place with his new trough. He looked very stylish beside his freshly painted trough.

But there was no mud to roll in. So the pig just stood beside his new trough and looked stylish.

Then the little woman bought the boys new suits. She bought stiff white shirts and new ties and shiny new shoes for the boys. They looked very stylish in their new clothes.

But the boys could not climb trees in their new clothes. They could not slide on the barn roof or play football in their new clothes. So they sat on the porch and looked stylish.

Then the little woman bought herself a new silk dress. She bought a gold pin with a ruby in it. She bought silk stockings and shoes with high heels. She had her hair curled and piled high on her head. She put some polish on her fingernails. She bought a tiny little hat with a curly feather. She sat in a chair on the porch and folded her hands and looked very, very stylish.

"My, but I am stylish," she said. "My, my, but we are all stylish. We look wonderful, we are so stylish. I wish someone important like the governor would come to call."

The little woman sat and sat and sat on the porch and looked stylish. But after a while the little woman got tired of sitting. She got tired of looking stylish.

"I would like to gather the eggs," she said. "I would like to milk the cow. I really should feed the pig. I wish I could wash the car. I am getting very hungry," she said. "I would like to get supper. But I can't in these clothes. I can't because I'm so stylish."

The little woman felt *very* unhappy.

Then she looked around at all her stylish family. They all looked unhappy. The cow was not eating. The dog was not fighting. The cat was not chasing mice. The duck was not catching bugs. The chickens were not scratching for worms. The pig was not rolling in the mud. The boys were not running and playing. Not one of them was doing what he wanted to do. Not one of them looked happy.

It was very quiet on the little woman's farm. There were no merry sounds of play and no pleasant sounds of happy voices.

The little woman took off the cow's stylish hat and hung it on a nail in the barn. She took off the dog's handsome harness and hung it on a hook by the back door. She took off the cat's beautiful ribbon and bells and hung them beside the dog's harness. She took the duck out of the clean clear pond and let him swim in the dirty pool on the pasture. She put the pig back in the mud hole. She took the leg bands off the hens and the rooster and hung them on a nail in the henhouse. She let the boys take off their new clothes and hang them in their closet.

Then the little woman took off her own fine

clothes. She put her hat with the curly feather on the shelf. She hung up her new silk dress.

Then she stirred up the fire and put on the kettle. She set the table and put some muffins in the oven to bake. She got her milking pail and her egg basket, and food for the pig.

And now the little woman could hear all the happy sounds of her animals. She could hear the boys laughing and shouting.

It sounded good to the little woman.

She thought of the cow's hat hanging in the barn. She thought of the dog's harness and the cat's ribbon and bells. She thought of the colored leg bands in the henhouse. She looked at the lovely clean pond and the pig's new trough. She thought of the boys' new suits and her own fine clothes.

"There they are," the little woman said, "when we need them. We can be stylish now whenever we want to. And when the governor comes to call, we'll use our stylish things. We'll be very, very stylish *WHEN WE HAVE TO.*"

SUSAN AND THE RAIN

by MADYE LEE CHASTAIN

Susan Amantha Cottonwood
   was a little girl
      who was always good—
         when
            the sun
               shone.

But when the clouds piled up in the sky
And began to rain—she would *cry!*
   And *cry* and *moan!*

Susan Amantha *hated* the rain.
She would press her nose to the windowpane
   And complain,
      And complain,
         And complain!

"There's *nothing* to do if I can't play outside.
If the sun was out, I'd take my doll for a ride,
I'd bounce my ball, I'd swing on the gate;
I'd go round the block on one roller skate!

146

But there's nothing to do in the whole wide world—
   When it rains!"

Now one summer she went to the country
   To visit her grandpapa,
And her uncles and aunts and cousins,
   And her grandmamma.

She played in the barn on the piles of hay,
She played in the meadow the livelong day.
The sun shone bright and Susan was gay!
But one day
     It *rained!*
        And Susan *complained!*

Her grandpapa was amazed to hear
So many complaints and he said, "I fear
You don't know why we have the rain
Or you *wouldn't* complain!"

"We have the rain to water the crops,
To make fine lettuce and big beet tops.
It makes the corn tall, row on row,
And the apples juicy and the blackberries grow.
It fills the rivers and streams and lakes.
It softens the soil the gardener rakes.

It washes the dust from all the leaves
And makes a song as it drips from the eaves.
Why, nothing would grow on our very own farm
If it didn't *rain*.
   Susan—*don't* complain!"

Susan Amantha Cottonwood
Told grandpapa that she understood,
But just the same
   It wasn't much fun
      When there was no sun!

Susan went home and though she *tried*,
Nevertheless, when it rained, she cried.
Until . . .
One day the postman rang the bell.
Mother opened the door and said, "Well, well!
Here's a package for Susan from Grandpapa."

When Susan got the strings untied
And opened the box, she found inside,
A bright red umbrella, shiny black boots
And a red plaid raincoat
With a rainhat to suit!

Well, the next time it rained
Did Susan complain?
      NO!

She put on her boots
And her raincoat and hat
And she took her umbrella and went spitty-spat
Out in the rain—
    And in all the puddles!

Rain thumped her umbrella,
Rain spattered her coat;
Each boot was as wet as a shiny black boat.
She splashed and she sploshed,
As happy as could be, and she said,
    "Why the rain *is* fun,
    And it's raining *just* for *me!*"

FIREFLY

by ELIZABETH MADOX ROBERTS

A little light is going by,
Is going up to see the sky
A little light with wings.

I never could have thought of it
To have a little bug all lit
And made to go on wings.

I SEE THE MOON

I see the moon
The moon sees me
God bless the moon
God bless me.

ON THE TOP OF THE HILL

by KATHRYN HITTE

Billy climbed the hill to the very top.
The top was tall and far away,
And the day was a very warm summer day,
And the hill was a long, long, hilly hill;
But he climbed and climbed till the top came near,
Till he came at last to the very top,
And there he stayed all the rest of the day.
He loved the hill and he stayed all day,
All day long on the top of the hill,
On the tall, far top of the hill.

Billy lay down in the grass on the hill.
The soft grass waved in the windy air.
It waved with the breeze and brushed his face.
He stretched his arms where the grass grew thick.
He loved the feel of the cool green grass.
He stayed all day in the soft, cool grass,
All day long in the grassy place
On the tall, far top of the hill.

There were animals living on the hill.
A rabbit scampered and flicked its ears.
It wiggled its nose and flicked its ears,
And hurried into its hole in the ground.
It lived in the ground on the hill.
A squirrel stood holding a nut in its paws.
Its bushy tail waved and it cocked its head.
It nibbled the nut and then ran up a tree.
It lived in a tree on the hill.
There were insects in the grass.
A grasshopper hopped through the grass.
Its coat was green and its legs were long.
It swung on the top of a blade of grass.
It lived in the grass on the hill.
A troop of ants came marching past.
They followed the leader through the grass,
In and out, and up and down,

Till they came to their little sandy home.
They lived in the earth on the hill.
Billy loved the creatures in the grass.
He stayed all day with his animal friends,
All day long with the small, good things
Who lived on the top of the hill,
On the tall, far top of the hill.

The sky was blue above the hill.
Above and around and all about
The sky was bright and very blue.
There were two white clouds in the bright blue sky.
They looked like cotton fluffs in the wind.
The wind blew the cotton clouds in the sky.
The wind that blew was part of the sky.
And the warm bright sun was part of the sky,
The sun that shone and warmed the hill.
When the night time came, the moon would shine,
And there would be stars shining over the hill;
And the moon and the stars were part of the sky.
Billy loved the sky, and he stayed all day
Thinking about it, and watching the clouds;
All day long underneath the sky,
That spread its blue above the hill,
Above the tall, far top of the hill.

Billy sat on the hill till the end of the day.
He knew that the hill would wait for him,
Wait and wait till he came again.
So he said goodbye to the things on the hill,
To all the things that he loved on the hill;
He said goodbye at the end of the day,
And he went down the hill to his home,
To his mother and daddy and home.
He went down the long, long, hilly hill,
Till the top got farther and farther away—
All the way down from the place on the top,
On the tall, far top of the hill!

THE TRAIN THAT WOULD NOT
STAY ON THE TRACK

by CAROLINE D. EMERSON

Once upon a time there was a train that was tired of staying on the track.

"Why must I run on a track all the days of my life?" asked the train.

"You had much better stay where you are," said the track. "I was laid for you to run on and you were made to run on me. Everything is better off in this world if it stays where it belongs."

But the train would not listen.

"I'm not going to stay here," he said and he jumped off the track and began to run along the road.

"Keep off!" cried the automobiles. "This road was made for us. Keep off! Keep off!"

"No such thing!" said the train, "there's plenty of room on the road for me."

He ran on down the road. He stopped at the houses for people and trunks and he stopped at the post office for the mail bags. He ran out to the barns for the milk. Everyone was delighted. It was much easier than to carry everything down to the station. But the train took so long that he never got to the end of his trip!

People waited for their trunks and they never came. The letters in the mail bags were so old that no one troubled to read them. The milk was sour and was no good to any one. People stopped putting their things on to the train and began to send them by automobile instead.

"There now," said the automobiles, "no one is using you any more. You should have stayed on your track as we told you to. The road is no place for you."

But the train refused to go back to his track. One day he saw a horse running across the fields.

"Why should I stay on a road?" asked the train. "That looks like fun."

He left the road and started off across the fields.

"You mustn't come here!" cried the horse, "this is my field. Keep off! Keep off!"

"No such thing," answered the train, "there's plenty of room in this field for me."

Bump, bump, bump went the train across the field until he came to a brook.

"How do I get over this?" asked the train.

"Jump," said the horse.

"I never jumped in my life," said the train, "I always have bridges laid down for me."

"Bridges?" laughed the horse. "You'd better go back where you belong. The track is the place for you."

But the train paid no attention to him for just then he heard an airplane up in the air.

"That looks like fun," said the train. "*Why* should I stay on the ground? I'm going to fly."

"Silly," said the horse, "you, who can't even jump a brook!"

The train tried to fly. He tried with his front wheels. He tried with his back wheels. He tried with *all* his wheels. He tried until he was tired.

"Well," said the train, "there appears to be something wrong. I can't fly. People won't ride on me when I bump across the fields and they won't send trunks and mail by me when I run on the road. They say I'm too slow. I don't seem to be good for anything! I might as well stay right here and let my fires go out. No one would miss me!"

The train felt lonely and discouraged. He felt he was no longer of any use in the world. Then an idea flashed through his steam pipes.

"I might go back to my tracks," he thought. "I wonder if they're still there?"

He crept across the field and down the road to the station. There lay the tracks right where he had left them, stretching off in both directions. They looked so safe and smooth! The train gave a great puff of happiness as he climbed back onto them.

"It's been lonely without you," said the tracks. "We were afraid we'd rust away with no one running over us."

At the station there were many people waiting and a pile of trunks and mail bags.

"This is just where I belong," whistled the train, cheerfully. And from that time on the little train could be seen every day running happily down the tracks, as smooth as could be.

GOOD NIGHT

by VICTOR HUGO

Good night! Good night!
Far flies the light;
But still God's love
Shall flame above,
Making all bright.
Good night! Good night!